ALEGRÍA
BY KILINA VELA

Order this book online at www.trafford.com
or email orders@trafford.com

Most Trafford titles are also available at major online book retailers.

Co-authored by Estevan Vela.
Edited by Estela Hernández-Robinson.
Cover Design Naun Ybarra.
Photography by Oded Moore & Naun Ybarra.
Foreword Estela Hernández-Robinson

Note for Librarians: A cataloguing record for this book is available from Library
and Archives Canada at www.collectionscanada.ca/amicus/index-e.html

Printed in Victoria, BC, Canada.

ISBN: 978-1-4251-8648-7 (sc)

*Our mission is to efficiently provide the world's finest, most comprehensive
book publishing service, enabling every author to experience success.
To find out how to publish your book, your way, and have it available
worldwide, visit us online at www.trafford.com*

Trafford rev. 9/18/2009

Trafford
PUBLISHING®

www.trafford.com

North America & International
toll-free: 1 888 232 4444 (USA & Canada)
phone: 250 383 6864 ♦ fax: 812 355 4082

ALEGRÍA

DEDICATION

To Kilina—loving daughter, granddaughter
and friend for without your love,
this story would not have been possible.

TABLE OF CONTENTS

ALEGRÍA

FOREWORD

I SAVED THE E-MAIL Steve Vela sent me on February 20, 2006 –
"Today you are in my prayers because I know Omar is in a better
place with Kilina. I dreamed about her on my birthday because that
was the only present I wanted, and she told me to listen because we
have the pictures and the memories—but the only way to communicate is through the voices we hear in our mind and heart. As long as
we believe, they will always be there to guide us to the end of our
days ..."

My nephew Omar had succumbed to Duchenne muscular dystro-
phy three days before; his daughter Kilina had lost her life in a freak
traffic accident the previous spring. Steve only knew Omar through
the stories I told him, yet his words were probably the most comfort-
ing that anyone gave me. I, on the other hand, was blessed to have met
and known Kilina—I was her teacher and family friend.

Estevan's book Alegría is a moving tribute to the daughter the Vela
family lost in such an untimely fashion. Mostly memoire, partly imag-
ined story, in Alegría Steve makes the supreme sacrifice any parent
would make and allegorically casts himself as the one who dies in the
accident. Kilina lives and the book is imbued with her shimmering
spirit and joie de vivre, her alegría de la vida.

Steve's literary voice shines through. In telling Kilina's story (including the warts and all), he reveals those ideas and issues which
are important to him and which were and would have been important
to his daughter. He uses language that is eloquent in its simplicity

and dialogue that is real and funny—his book is eminently readable. Kilina knew her dad's love of writing and gift for storytelling. She would be so proud of how well he has listened to her voice in his mind and heart.

Estela Hernández-Robinson
English Teacher
Family Friend

PROLOGUE

It was almost nine o'clock PST at Conroy's Flowers when Kilina Vela, 19-year-old coed, called Vanessa Garcia, her roommate at Cal State University, Long Beach on her cell phone. Vanessa answered in an anxious tone:

"What time do you get off work?"

"I'm almost done. I'll be there in 15 to pick you girls up!"

"Take your time. We're already ready!"

Kilina was five foot two. She had a heart shaped face with hazel eyes that revealed the childlike quality of her personality. Her long brown hair fell off her shoulders in a rush. She was shapely but slender at 105 pounds, and the way she walked told everyone she came in contact with that there was no nonsense about her.

Kilina finished cleaning the counters. She counted the receipts in the cash register. She checked her cell phone for any messages and she shuffled through her purse to make sure she had her car keys. Then she remembered she wasn't in her car because she had left it in Chula Vista to get repaired. "Whew—one less thing to worry about," she thought to herself. She was about to call Vanessa on the phone again when her phone rang.

"It's me Girl—we're outside in the car waiting for you."

"I need to go back to the crib to get my things!" Kilina responded.

"That's okay—we brought your *trapos* and your shoes with us. You can dress in the car, or we'll stop at the rest area at San Onofre so you can change."

"Did you bring my green shoes with the laces in front?"

"Of course! *Que piensas!*"

""Okay—but I'll drive. That way we'll get there faster."

On the way, after she changed into her party clothes. Kilina answered her phone three times and called her boyfriend Kariff once to tell him he needed to be ready when they got to his house. "You better be out of the shower by then!" Kariff said he would be ready. Forty-five minutes later, when Vanessa's red Jetta passed over the San Diego County line, Kilina told the girls, Hawaii and Erin, that they would be going to a *quinceañera* in *Tijuana*. It was her childhood friend Victor's sister's 15th birthday. It was a coming-of-age party to announce a young girl's welcoming into society. In so many words, she explained that a *quinceañera* is similar to a sweet sixteen party in the United States.

The Jetta crossed Sweetwater River and Kilina sighed deeply because she felt like she was already home. When the girls got to the H Street Bridge in Chula Vista, they could see the red lights flashing and the big red fire truck on the side of the road. The police had set out flares on the freeway to divert the traffic away from the accident. Curiously there seemed to be only one vehicle involved.

"Probably, a drunk driver," one of the girls thought out loud.

CHAPTER 1

THE TOP OF THE FERRIS WHEEL

KILINA'S YOUNGER SISTER KARINA told her dad that she was invited to the movies by her best buddy Carol. They were going to see Natalie Babbit's "Tuck Everlasting" the story about a family that achieves immortality by drinking from the Fountain of Youth. Her dad, Estevan, a 57 year old English teacher at Otay Ranch High School, told her that he had passes from the teacher's union so she wouldn't have to pay the $9.50 ticket price.

"Karina—you better be ready in fifteen minutes; otherwise, you're going to miss the best part of the movie."

"All right, dad," Karina moaned.

When Estevan got into the green Ford Explorer, his first reaction was to remain silent because Karina had been on his nerves all day long by asking: "What should I wear? Was it going to be hot or cold? Was the movie rated R or PG13?" He was kind of at the end of his rope; then, he thought to himself, "I've got one daughter at home with her son. My son is at home with his wife. I have another daughter at Cal State Long Beach. My wife is doing her caregiver job in La Jolla. This is the only person I have close to me, here and now, for better or for worse—God give me patience!"

"Karina—remember the story Tuck Everlasting?"

"Yeah, I remember, dad."

"So . . . It's kind of cool that they made it into a movie?"

"I know. I was thinking about the same thing. Who would have believed that they would have done that so soon after the book came out!"

"Actually, the book was written in 1975."

"Wow, I wasn't even born yet."

"You know, Karina, what my favorite part of the book is?"

"What was it, dad?"

"It's the very first line of the book—'The first week of August hangs at the very top of summer . . . the top of the live long year, like the highest seat of the Ferris wheel when it pauses in its turning.'"

"You like Ferris wheels?"

"I guess so, but what I like even more is the picture it paints inside my head. It seems like that's an important thing to remember in the grand scheme of things."

Father and daughter both laughed at the thought as they arrived at the entrance of the Regal Cinemas in Chula Vista. Carol and her father were already waiting, so Estevan stopped to drop Karina off and told her he would be back to pick her up at 11:30 PM.

"Don't leave without a kiss," Karina told him.

Estevan leaned over to kiss his daughter. Neither one of them knew it would be the last time they would see each other.

Very few accidents make real sense. For example, a split second can make all the difference in the world. Some people say it's destiny, or rotten luck. Some people want to believe it's God's providence. It's probably a combination of both-and a lot of other things that we just don't understand. That night when Estevan drove home alone, he got on the H Street Bridge and waited his turn to go south on Interstate 805. He moved on to the freeway briskly, which was his regular routine. As he picked up speed, he crossed over two lanes. Without noticing where it came from, a 350 Series steel belted radial tire from a blue Dodge Ram pickup going northbound came off the front wheel of the truck. It picked up speed as it ran toward the embankment and caromed high into the air over the center divide and fell directly into the driver's side windshield of Estevan's green Explorer killing him instantly.

CHAPTER 2

BAD NEWS

THE PARAMEDICS were on the scene at 9:45 PM. Only good NEWS travels at the speed of snail mail. The body was pronounced dead at 9:55 PM. The radio call went out to Chula Vista Fire Station 29, so that the relatives could be informed. Fernando Felix, who was Estevan Vela's son-in-law worked at the fire station during the day, so the nightshift relayed the message to him promptly. The first call went out to Evangelina, Estevan's wife. It was 10:15 PM and the coroner in charge spoke cautiously and deliberately to the woman on the phone. Only Kilina's recorded message on the answering machine responded at the Vela residence: "We're not home right now. Please leave us a message! *Que dios les bendiga!*"

The paramedics arrived at Fernando Felix's residence at 555 Falcon Lane to deliver the bad NEWS around 11:05 PM. Melody Vela answered the door:

"Are you Mrs. Felix?

"Yes—May I help you? Are you looking for my husband, Fernando?"

"Mrs. Felix. Your father's name is Estevan Vela? He lives at 1569 Skylark Way in Chula Vista?"

"The same!"

"We regret to inform you that your father has been injured in a serious accident."

At this point Fernando had joined his wife at the threshold of their home.

"Oh my God! Are you sure? Is he still alive?"

"We wouldn't be here unless it was true, ma'am. He was listed in critical condition at the scene. You'll have to call the hospital to get an update."

"Have you notified anyone else?"

"No ma'am, only you."

"Okay—okay. Let me think. I've got to let the rest of the family know."

"Can we assist you by notifying the rest of the family?"

"No! I can do that. I need a few minutes to gather my thoughts to know what I'm going to tell them."

"Fernando—use your contacts to find out how father is doing."

Fernando used his cell phone to call the Trauma Center at UCSD Medical Center in Hillcrest. After transferring from the switchboard, the doctor answered on the other end.

"Are you a relative?"

"Yes—I'm his son."

"I regret to inform you that your father passed away at 9:55 PM."

Fernando looked thunderstruck. He looked into his wife's eyes and said, "He's gone!"

By this time Kilina had arrived at Kariff's condo, but he was still in the shower. The red Jetta was parked outside his house and Kilina alerted him on her cell phone three times in a row to let him know they were waiting for him. When Kariff finally came to the door, the girls looked chagrined.

"I thought we agreed that you would be ready! The party already started an hour ago!" Kariff was still drying his lion's head of hair.

"Kilina—you know that nothing happens in the first hour anyway!"

"That's not the point! By the time we get there, it will be two hours!"

"Okay, okay. I'll hurry up."

The full load of friends boarded the Jetta on their way to *Tijuana* to the *quinceañera*. They crossed the border at 10:30 PM and wound their way around *Pueblo Amigo* to get to their destination. Once they parked the Jetta on their way to the party, they proceeded to *Las Americas* social hall where the event was taking place. Kilina's phone rang twice, but when she tried to answer it, the screen only read "Out of Service".

CHAPTER 3

FAMILY TIES

THE SECOND CALL went out to Estevan's son, Stevan Junior, from his sister Melody at 10:20 PM: "Are you driving?"

"No, we just got home. What's the matter?"

"Father was in a car accident. He didn't suffer. He's passed on . . . We are here at the house. Have you heard from Kilina?"

"Oh my God, Melody! How did it happen?" Stevan inquired.

"All we know right now is there was a tire from another car that was on the scene. Apparently, it came off the other car's wheel."

"I'll be over as soon as I can get myself together."

"Stevan's wife Malú asked 'What happened?'"

"My dad—he was in an accident!"

"How did he die?"

"How did you know he was killed?"

"You're as pale as a sheet, and you know I sense things before they happen. I've had a strange feeling all night."

"We need to dress in something more comfortable. We're going over to Fernando and Melody's to find out what happens next."

"Does your mom and your sisters know?"

"I don't know who knows—that's why we need to get over there."

Steve and Malú dressed and got into the car at 10:45 PM. There was no verbal communication between them, but their silence spoke volumes of how they felt. When they arrived at their destination, they

paused briefly to think about what to say. Fernando greeted them at the door.

"It isn't fair," Fernando said barely speaking as he embraced Steve. Melody came up from behind and hugged them both.

"Have you told Kilina yet?" Do either of you know if Karina was in the car with him?"

"I didn't even ask about Karina, but the paramedics didn't say anything about a second person in the car—we better call the house to see if she is there," Melody answered.

"Will you call mom—or do you want me to call her?" Steve asked.

"You do it. I don't know what to tell her."

"Okay. Hand me the phone."

Steve dialed the numbers in slow motion 8 9 1-5 6 4 6. His mother spoke as if waking from a deep sleep on the other end: "*Que pasó, Guy?*"

"Mom. *Estas despierta?*"

"*Si, que pasó?*"

"Father had an accident. We want you to come and be with us."

"I can't right now. There's no one here to take care of the viejito—it's the middle of the night—I'll be there first thing in the morning."

"Mamá. We need you now! The morning will be too late."

"I just can't right now."

"Mom—I didn't want to have to tell you on the phone . . . Father's gone! He was killed in a car accident a little while ago."

A little sob came over the phone. All she said was, "I felt like something was wrong, so I've been praying all night. I'll see what I can do."

⁘

Melody thought the last piece of the puzzle was letting her little sisters know, but first she had to find Karina. Carol's dad called her house, but when no one answered, he decided to take Karina home. When Karina walked through the front door, Melody's call went through.

"Hello?" Karina asked into the receiver.

"Where were you?" Melody said.

"I was at the movies—with Carol!"

"Did dad know you were at the movies?"

"He dropped me off, but he didn't come back to pick me up."

Suddenly, it became perfectly clear to Melody what had happened that night. Their father had probably told Karina he would wait outside the theater when she got out. He was always at the right spot at the right time.

"Karina. Dad was in an accident."

"Is he okay?"

"I'll come over in a few minutes to pick you up. I'll tell you all about it then."

"Okay."

A few minutes later, Melody was in front of the house. She had wanted to bring her two-year old son Felix to keep her company because this was not an easy thing to do, but he had fallen asleep on the couch from running around the room. When she walked up to the door, she was thinking of what she wanted to say when Karina opened the door.

"Melody. He's not coming back from the hospital, huh?" Melody hugged her little sister. "No—he's gone."

"Melody. Can I stay with you?"

"Yeah, come on—I'll take you home."

It was now close to daybreak. All attempts to reach Kilina were futile. The phone messages all read "Out of Service". Melody knew that she probably had gone to stay at Kariff's house. She also knew she had to get a hold of her somehow. She decided to try one last time, but before she could do that, her phone rang: "Melody—what happened? Why were you calling me all night?" Kilina's voice resonated on the other end.

"I need you to get your butt home right now!"

"Why? What's the matter?" Kilina said anxiously.

"It's father—he's been in an accident."

"I'll be there as soon as I can get dressed," she muttered.

When Kilina arrived, the whole family was sitting on the sofa exhausted from the shock and grief. Obviously, this had been a long night. It was also painfully clear that whatever had happened, her father wasn't coming back any time soon. Kilina was the sentimental one in the family, so the tears began to roll down her cheeks. "What happened?" was all she could say. The rest of the family came to hug her.

"We don't know all of the specifics—apparently, dad was coming home from the movies and something, or someone hit his car," Steve said. "That's all we know for now."

Kilina was distraught. She had a stomachache all night. She thought it was cramps—but it wasn't that time of the month. Even at the *quince* she wasn't able to get comfortable; she got mad at Kariff for no apparent reason when they came back from the party crossing the border. They had all sprawled out on the living room floor in front of the TV at Kariff's when they got to the condo—but Kilina wasn't able to sleep. When the call to Melody went through, she had barely slept for a half hour. Now she thought about her Nany, her grandmother, and how she would be the one to tell her about her beloved son.

CHAPTER 4
TOUGH LOVE

WHEN THEY ARRIVED at Nany's house, Kilina knocked on the door. Nany was still in her robe and nightcap. She got up to hug Kilina as she came to the glass door: "What's the matter, hun?"

"Nany. I don't know how to say it—we lost dad last night!"

"What? No, no, no . . . I knew something was wrong when I saw you all at the door."

They all embraced as if to hold one another up with the weight of the unfortunate NEWS. At times like these, words get stuck to the roof of your mouth like peanut butter. How can you speak the unspeakable? Tragedy has a language all its own and it can't be interpreted with words. They cried out loud. When the tears subsided, Nany spoke first: "What happened?"

Kilina told her what she knew, "We are not really sure what happened. All we know is that he was coming home from dropping Karina off at the movies. Something—a tire flew over the embankment and crushed him in the seat of his truck."

"Nobody else was hurt?" Nany wondered out loud.

"No—as far as we can tell. He was the only one in the accident."

"It must have been his time," Steve muttered.

"What do you children need me to do?" Nany inquired.

"Nothing right now," Kilina said. Melody's taking care of the arrangements . . . Nany can I stay with you a little while—I haven't slept all night. I could really use a few hours rest."

"Of course you can," her grandmother whispered.

The rest of the family gave their condolences and quietly slipped out of the side door. Kilina went in the back room and lied down to rest. She fell asleep as soon as her head hit the pillow.

When Kilina woke up, she squinted the last clump of tears and sleep out of her eyes and she told her grandmother, "I just need to walk and think a little while." Then she walked quietly and deliberately out of Nany's trailer. She began walking in the direction of her home. At first, she thought about how maybe this was all a bad dream. Maybe she would wake up and everything would be normal again; but, somehow, she knew it wouldn't happen this way. Then she thought about how it happened. Why did her dad have to die the way he did? Did he ask God to end his life? Did he have a chance to think about it before it happened? What was the purpose of living a life left unfinished? All these questions had no definite answers. She felt like going back to sleep and dream about her dad so that he could answer her questions; however, in the next few days, she found out she couldn't dream about him at all.

When she got home, Kariff was waiting for her in his car impatiently. "Why didn't you call me to come get you?" he said.

"I just needed time to be with my Nany," she responded.

"Well—Melody has been calling me to ask me where you were. She told me to go get you a couple of times, but I told her I couldn't—so you call her."

"I'll call her, but not right now. I just need you to hold me for a little while."

"We need to go get your car today. It's already fixed. It was the dashboard computer . . . "

Kilina remembered that her dad had offered to let her take his car to Long Beach, so she wouldn't be without a car that week. She thought to herself that maybe what happened wouldn't have happened if she had her dad's car. It was no use. Like her father used to say, "Hindsight is always 20/20." Then it hit her like a lightening bolt. The sirens. , The fire truck, the paramedics—that was the accident they had seen on their way to pick up Kariff. She started to cry. "What's the matter?" Kariff asked apologetically.

I saw the accident on the way to your house last night. Erin said it was probably a drunk driver. It was my dad. If I had stopped . . . "

"There is no way you could have known it was your dad."

"But my dad would have stopped if he thought it were me," Kilina said.

"You don't know that. Beside your dad wouldn't have wanted you to stop—so you need to stop feeling guilty about it."

Kilina felt chagrined at this last remark, but she knew Kariff. It wasn't malicious—it was just his way of trying to comfort her and it wasn't working. "Call Melody and tell her we will be over there in five minutes."

When they arrived at Melody's, there were a lot of family and friends sitting around. She didn't have to greet anyone. They all came up to her and gave her their condolences. They told her how sorry they were and they would pray for her dad and for her. All she could think about was that her dad spent zero hours in prayer—less than he spent at church and that brought a smile to her face. Her dad once told her that she could find God anywhere. "God doesn't frequent churches," he once said. "He would much rather go to a dance or see a ball game." She could picture her father laughing when he said it. Before she could finish enjoying the moment, Melody pulled her aside and said, "Let's talk in my bedroom."

When the family was in the bedroom together, they sat on the floor facing each other. Melody spoke first: "We need to get an attorney," she blurted out.

"What do we need an attorney for?" her mother mused.

"Because we don't know who or what caused the accident, or who the other people are involved," Steve chimed in.

"How is an attorney going to fix this?" Kilina wanted to know—a little annoyed.

Fernando said, "We don't know what caused the wheel to come off of the car. But if we don't take action—somebody else will."

"I don't understand—this was an accident, right?" Kilina said poignantly.

"Yes," Melody reiterated.

"Then I don't understand. What possible good can retaining an attorney do in this case?" Kilina used her scolding voice now.

"We need to find out what caused the tire to come off of the truck," Steve answered.

"And if we don't?" Kilina responded.

"Then someone can suggest that this was as much father's fault as the driver who lost the tire," Fernando spoke out.

"Yo pienso que estan desperdiciando su tiempo," Evangelina spoke in a commanding tone.

"No. We are not wasting our time," Melody said taking control of the conversation " . . . because we will find out the truth."

"Who is going to pay for the attorney, Melody?" Kilina wanted to know.

"Normally, any attorney who would represent us will take this on a contingency basis," Steve surmised.

"Que quiere decir eso?" their mother wanted to know.

"What it means mother is that the attorney takes a percentage of what we get if there is a settlement. If there is no legal process, then we don't owe the attorney anything," Melody explained.

"Then what is the purpose," her mother inquired.

"The purpose is to pay for funeral expenses and any pain and suffering the family endures," Fernando told her.

"It just seems too prosaic for dad. If he were here, getting an attorney would have been the last thing on his mind. What are we doing for his services?" Kilina wanted to know.

"We are going to do a celebration of life—like we did for our grandfather, Papí," Steve said.

"It seems like that should be our first priority right now," Kilina said barely audible because of the knot in her throat.

"We will revisit this conversation later on," Melody added.

The next few days were hectic. On Monday the family went to see Araceli Ramirez who worked for Humphrey's Mortuary because she was a close friend who could expedite the process. She was able to call the morgue, secure the body and have their father's remains cremated by the following Saturday. Melody gave a press release inviting everybody to the service on the same day. Mom arranged for a memorial service at the church, which was agreed on by consensus—even though Kilina objected more than once. Everyone had a function and a phone list of people to invite to the funeral. The family came together like no other time in their short existence to make everyone in attendance feel welcome.

On the day of the event, twelve hundred people showed up. There were friends of the family, ex-students from twenty-two years in the classroom, doctors, dentists, accountants and attorneys—people from all walks of life. A few people spoke about Estevan and his contributions to the community, but mostly people came to offer their condolences. There was too much food. People ate like eating was going out of style. At times, people were rude and obnoxious because they claimed to be more of a friend, or closer as a relative, which made this seem like it was more of a wedding than a funeral. More than one person made the statement that Estevan wouldn't have wanted the people to be contrite or humble because that wasn't his style either.

CHAPTER 5
DECISIONS

The next few weeks were like no other time in the Vela family. Kilina wanted to seriously drop out of school, but she knew deep down that that would have upset her father. What it boiled down to was that Kilina was like her mom in some ways because she liked to change things versus her dad who preferred to leave things the way they were. One time before, when she didn't know what she wanted to do, they had this conversation:

"What do you plan to do if you don't go to school?" her father asked her.

"I'm going to take a sabbatical, dad." Kilina replied.

"That's not what I'm hearing. You just explained that you want to drop out of your classes at Long Beach and enroll in IEU to take computer programming classes."

Kilina who was visibly flustered said, "Yes—because that will give me time to make the right decision about what to do in the future."

"Don't you understand, my love, you are at the right place at the right time—and you have plenty of time to make the right choices. So, maybe it takes you another year or three—it doesn't matter. God put you where you are for a reason. It's all about networking right now. Maybe it doesn't feel right to you, but give it some time. You will know what you want to do with your life when the right thing comes along."

"That sounds redundant, dad! How will I know what the right thing is if I stay in one place. It just doesn't make sense to me. At least if I try something different, I'll have some basis for comparison," she retorted.

"That's my point! By trying something different from the course of action you are on—you're out of sync and you've lost your focus on what you're doing today. People who are constantly changing majors, changing their mind, changing their outlook are immature. People who get up every day and don't know what they want, but are determined to find out, they are on their destined path," Estevan explained.

"Dad—sometimes you don't make any sense to me at all, but I still love you anyways," Kilina smiled.

"Me too," was all he said.

One day, while Kariff and Kilina were in the drugstore looking for some toiletries, a big smile came over Kilina's face when the cashier tapped her on the shoulder and said, "Look—there is a beautiful butterfly fluttering over aisle 17." To everyone in the store, it was just a butterfly, but to Kilina, it was a way for her dad to communicate to her that he was all right.

As they left the store, Kilina was still smiling because of the butterfly; however, the problem with epiphanies is they have a bad habit of disappearing with a change of scenery.

"What am I supposed to do now?" Kilina asked Kariff.

"I don't know—what do you want to do?" Kariff inquired.

"On the one hand, I feel like I owe it to my dad to stay in school and finish what I started; however, I still can't get over the feeling that I'm spinning my wheels—I'm not going anywhere!"

"Why do you have to go ANYWHERE? Why can't you just stay here and finish up at San Diego State?"

"You know what? That's exactly what I'm going to do. I'm going to put in my transfer as soon as I get back to Long Beach."

"Don't you think you should talk to your mom about it," Kariff wondered.

"I've already spoken to my mom—*ya la conoces*. All she said to me was that I would not have the same amount of freedom that I have at Long Beach. What I liked about what she said was that I would pay her rent, and that she would create a savings account based on what I give her, so that I would have money once I graduated. That sounds like a good idea—don't you think?"

"You mean she's going to charge you rent, but she's gonna give you the money?"

"It's kind of too good to be true, but that's what she said."

"Maybe you ought to talk to Melody and find out what she thinks about it," Kariff suggested.

"I already know what Melody is going to say: She'll say, 'Why don't you come live with me and I'll offer you the same deal; except, at our house, you'll still have your freedom.'"

"*Y porque NO?*" Kariff wanted to know.

"I know it sounds strange, but the only reason I feel I need to come home is—I miss my dad. I kinda feel like in some way, he'll be there to watch over me. I know it sounds silly, but I know my dad. He will find some way to be there when I need him the most. He won't ever leave me alone."

"You're not alone. I'm here with you, Kilina," Kariff said.

"I know—but this is different. When I talk to my dad, I know there is nothing to fear, no one to judge me. I know he'll guide me in the right direction."

Kariff wondered out loud again, half as a question, half as a reply, "Maybe what you feel is your depression talking."

Kilina felt the blood rush to her face, but she remained calm, "No—I know it's not that because I've been depressed before, and believe me—it doesn't feel like this; in fact, I feel remarkably calm. I know that's my dad lending a helping hand. It's as if he wants me to know that everything is going to be okay. That's why it's so important that I be at home. That way I can relay what I feel to my sisters and brother; plus, I want him to know that I miss him—just the way he was always there for me."

MAKING THE MINUTES COUNT

As the days rolled by, so did the Vela's lives. No one did much of anything differently than before. Kilina commuted back and forth from Long Beach waiting to transfer to San Diego State University in the fall. Steve returned to his job at Migrant Glass and plunged headlong into his work, but began taking online courses through University of Phoenix to complete his bachelor's degree in administration. Karina returned to school, but her behavior at home changed. She claimed she heard funny noises and saw shadows in the corner of her room at night, so her mom let her sleep in her queen size bed sometimes. Melody was a basket case because she tried to be strong for everyone. Some days she would create projects in which everyone in the family would have a task to complete, like moving her office from Lemon Grove to San Ysidro. Other times, she created opportunities for the family to get together to play Bunko or Scattegories. If anything, the family's energy level increased through the loss of their father. It was like they needed to make every minute count to honor their father's memory. The attorneys told them to be patient because the people that installed the tire were really the ones at fault, but their business didn't have any insurance to cover the Vela's claim, which only added to the conundrum.

Every little thing reminded Kilina of her dad. The alarm waking her up in the morning, the newspaper he used to read lying on the kitchen table and even the songs they used to listen to on the car radio. She remembered how he imitated Louie "Satchmo" Armstrong's deep baritone voice on "It's A Wonderful World": "I see trees of green— red roses too. I see 'em bloomin' for me and for you—and I think to myself—what a wonderful world."

Two weeks had passed when Kariff called Kilina on her cell phone to ask if she would meet him at his condo. It was early Friday morning. She had to ask for a half day off from her job at the flower shop to take care of a traffic ticket in downtown Long Beach for taking the express-way without having any money to pay the toll; and then drive to San Ysidro, which was an hour and a half away to make the rendezvous. Kariff was waiting with his arms crossed outside of the condo. Kilina suggested that they go for a walk on the Silver Strand in Imperial Beach, but Kariff claimed that the sand would be like sandpaper under their feet. They both laughed at the awkwardness of their conversation.

As they walked into the living room, she took him by the hand and they stood face to face for an instant before their lips locked in a firm but passionate kiss. They had played the game before—just not in the same sequence. She squeezed his hand and they walked deliberately toward his aunt's bedroom. As Kilina worked at the buttons on his jeans, Kariff unbuttoned her blouse. She drooped her fragile arms and let the shirt drop to the floor. Her breasts swelled beneath her bra, so he hurried to unfasten it. Her breasts were white and delicate and he bowed to taste them. Suddenly, they were both naked on top of the covers. Kariff's *bendición* was hard and ready to explode, but for some odd reason, he froze before penetrating her. After what seemed to be an eternity, he stopped kissing her.

"What's the matter?" she said. "Are you afraid? Do you need protection?"

"Why did your father send you away to Monterrey?"

Kilina moved from underneath his grasp and moved her arms so they circled in a locked position across her knees, How in the hell should I know!" she retorted. "Man—you really know how to spoil the mood—*dios mio!* Why would you care about that at a time like this?"

"I don't know. Don't be mad at me—it's like I can feel your dad's eyes on the back of my neck. I can't explain it! It felt like an electric shock going through my body, which felt like the cold water of the Pacific Ocean running across my spine," he said.

Kilina didn't know whether to laugh or cry, "I told you we should have gone for a walk on the beach. At least that way, you would have had an excuse for feeling the Pacific Ocean!"

Kariff's inspiration had gone limp.

"I don't know why my dad sent me away! I guess he thought it was a good idea at the time. Maybe he thought that if I stayed at home, I would end up running away with Adrian—my old boyfriend. In any case, he did me a favor. I got to travel. I met some new friends. I got to grow up at a time when I didn't have any other options," she said as she slowly reached for her blouse on the floor and began covering her delicate shoulders. "In any case, I'm kind of glad my dad sent me away because I got used to not seeing his smiling face all the time. It doesn't make it any easier to think about him being gone—it just makes it clear that he always had my back—even when he wasn't around to look after me; and now, he's still trying from a zillion miles away," she said as she buttoned the last fastener on her Levi's.

When the young couple left the condo, they walked silently to the car and—even after they had been driving for a while—suddenly, they saw them. At first it was a cluster, then it was a swarm of butterflies coming from the backyards of every house up ahead. Kilina pointed them out to Kariff:

"Look," she said. As they watched, thousands of butterflies came from everywhere. "See I told you your dad was trying to communicate with me," she chimed through her tears of joy and laughter.

Kariff was so mesmerized; he couldn't bring himself to speak. Finally, Kilina broke their silence, "Where are we going?"

"I thought you said you wanted to be close to the Pacific Ocean?"

"You're such a *pendejo* sometimes," Kilina said laughing out loud.

"Well, that's what you said!" Kariff explained jokingly.

"Oh my God! Remind me not to use figurative language around you any more unless I want to go insane," Kilina let her laugh role whole-heartedly.

CHAPTER 7

REMEMBERING THE FUN STUFF

THREE MONTHS to the day that Estevan passed away, Nany took ill. The first they knew was when Estevan's brother Martin called his nephew Steve in the middle of the night to tell him that his mom had apparently had a stroke. He called 911 and they had rushed her to Mercy Hospital. They found a tumor in her upper left thigh about the size of an orange, which was obstructing the circulation to her lower extremities. She had very little feeling in her feet. The tumor was deemed inoperable because it was located inside of her pelvis. The prognosis was to treat it with radiation and chemotherapy as a last resort. They eventually moved Nany to a convalescent home— Friendship Manor it was called. This posed a problem for Kilina because she felt like she should be with her Nany during her treatments; however, she could only do it once a week when she came home on Fridays from school. Instead, she called her grandmother every day about the same time in the morning to see how she was feeling and to hear her voice: "I'm okay, Hun. Gotta stay in there and pitch!"

One of the ways Kilina was helpful was to stay after the therapy and talk to Nany about her dad. The conversations that followed were usually about something Nany remembered about her son: "What do you remember most about my dad when he was a little boy?" Kilina asked.

"Well—let's see now. I remember he was always polite and very well behaved," Nany smiled.

"I would imagine you would say that about your son . . . I want to know about the fun stuff?"

"Oh, the fun stuff. Okay, Hun, well, I remember one time when he was in the shoe store across the street from where we lived. He was looking at some cowboy boots when another little boy came up to him. Your dad looked him straight in the eye and said, 'Are you looking for some boots? If you try 'em, you'll buy 'em!' That was so cute!"

"I can't imagine my dad being cute. You know, he was smiling all the time, but I can't really say it was cute," Kilina mused.

"You'll understand what I mean one of these days when you have a son. Everything they do is cute. Well, most of the time it is," Nany said laughing.

"Did he ever get into trouble?" Kilina wanted to know.

"Well, sure he did. I remember his dad, Alfonso, told him that he could dive off of the BIG pier because the current wasn't very strong there, but he should stay away from the little pier because he would be jumping right into the rapids. So one day, an older boy, Antonio Flores challenged your dad—that if he were a really good swimmer, he could swim faster than the current and get to the other side where Antonio stood. Well, your father couldn't say 'No' to a challenge, so he jumped headlong into the rapids. He swam really fast at first; then, he got tired and the current took him into the *remolinos*—the whirlpool caught him. The harder he swam, the more the vicious undertow began dragging him down."

"What happened, Nany?"

"Well, your grandfather watched from the shoreline, but he was paralyzed with shock from seeing your dad beginning to drown. Some other fishermen got into a skiff and rowed out to the whirlpool and saved him. When your father got back to shore, your Papi took a belt to him—I thought he was going to kill him for disobeying."

"What did my dad do?" Kilina asked.

"You know he never said anything about it, but I know it tore him up inside. He felt like your grandfather, his dad, had let him down because on top of the fact that he almost drowned, he suffered the worst humiliation of his life because he was beaten until he was raw."

"Did Papi ever apologize to him?" Kilina wanted to know.

"You know, I don't think he did. In your grandfather's mind, he was only doing what a father should do to teach his son a lesson. Nevertheless, I don't think your dad ever forgave him for that."

"I bet if he were alive today, he would."

"Why do you say that, Love?"

"Because now he would understand what it is like to be a father."

"Touché!"

On another occasion, the conversation drifted to what Nany thought about her when she was little. "You were such a precocious child," Nany offered.

"What does that mean, Nany?"

"It means that you were always mature for your age. You never liked hanging out with anyone who was younger than you."

"I used to hang out with my cousin, Lorena, a lot," Kilina interjected.

"Was she younger or older than you?"

"She was a year and a half older!"

"Now you know what precocious means."

"I love you, Nany."

"I love you too, doll."

≈≈≈

It was in the fall that Nany passed away. Everyone was saddened by her passing, but nobody more than Kilina because she felt like she had lost part of her soul with the death of her dad. Nany took what was left of her desire to 'Stay in there and pitch' every day—no doubt about it.

CHAPTER 8

CIRCUMSPECTION

WHAT KILINA MISSED most about her grandmother was her ability to listen without being judgmental. Not that she didn't have an opinion about almost everything that happened, but Nany could be absolutely impartial toward the side you were defending. For example, when Kilina told her Nany about why Kariff's aunt was mad at his best friend, René, Nany said, maybe she was just using René as an excuse so she wouldn't have to be mad at Kariff. That didn't make any sense to Kilina at first; but, after awhile, she understood what Nany was suggesting. That is: "When you're mad at a person who is totally oblivious to how you feel, or what you think, it doesn't do any good to stay angry with the person—it genuinely won't make a difference. However, if you can bring attention to your frustration by redirecting your anger, or aggravation, toward someone who your target person cares about—you can at least make a case for your point of view."

After her father died, Nany became Kilina's confidant—someone to trust and bring comfort to her when everything else seemed lost. Now Kilina had lost her soul mate, someone she suffered in silence with. She enjoyed Nany's company, especially on rainy days because she talked about San Quintin and her father as a little boy. It helped her make the connection between her father's personality and the way he transmitted those same traits to her, naturally and nurturing. She understood why she couldn't turn down a challenge that was within good reason, like tackling a puzzle or a word problem that everyone else had given up on. It also explained how she could turn her back and walk away from somebody who wanted to get in her face or start a fight. Most of all, she understood how her father could be the most generous person on the face of the earth, but be so stingy with his time. Why? It was because Kilina was like that, too.

One of the things that Nany confided in Kilina was that her mother had told her a story about Louise's dad (Louise was Nany's half sister; they had the same mother, but different fathers.) Louise had always bragged about what a great man her father was to her sister, and Nany never disputed it. However, one time, when Nany was alone with Granny Chock, her mother told her that she had caught Grandpa in bed with her Cousin May who had come to stay with them for a short time because of her illness. Louise's dad passed away in the fall of that year, so nothing else was said about it. The remarkable thing was that Nany had kept this secret for 75 years without saying anything to anybody. Kilina thought it was admirable, but sad that someone could hold on to a secret so tight—just so it wouldn't cause harm to the people they loved. It made her wonder if her dad had secrets that he took with him to the grave also. Then she remembered a conversation that they had when she was about ten years old. It was when they were driving back from San Quintin where her grandparents lived. The topic of conversation was something about how well her dad knew all his kids and how well they knew him:

"You know, Kilina, you are the one who will have to take care of me when I get old!"

"Why do you say that, dad?"

"Well—mostly because you're the only one who truly understands how I feel about things."

The sadness of his words overcame her and she began to cry: "Why are you thinking about getting old, dad?"

"I really don't know. I guess in part because I see your Papí. Nothing seems to make him happy anymore . . . At least part of that is because he never opens up to anyone—least of all to me. I don't want to be like that. I feel like I can talk to you about anything at any time for any reason—and you'll always tell me the truth. Nobody else in the family seems to understand that."

"Melody, Stevan and Karina love you too," Kilina told him.

"I know they do, but nobody loves me like you do—and that's the truth."

Kilina understood now about what the "truth" meant. It was kind of your own personal belief. Her dad had to feel loved and respected by all his kids, but he felt understood by Kilina more because she was the most like him—that was the truth.

CHAPTER 9

SIBLINGS

MY PARENTS LOVED to tell the story of how I was conceived. According to them, they had pretty much decided that they weren't going to have any more kids because my dad didn't want to be an "old fart with little kids", like his father while he was growing up. Nevertheless, my parents got involved with a youth group at their church, and the coordinator took them to see a film sponsored by Pro-Life, anti-abortionists in San Diego. That kind of settled the debate on whether or not they should have more children; however, my dad liked to tell the story about how I was conceived after an all night drinking party where both of my parents got thrashed. Anyway, it gave me a good excuse to become a party girl later on in my adolescence.

I have to say that I had a pretty normal childhood. I was always curious and all of my teachers loved me growing up in elementary school. I considered myself a little bit shy, but to hear my teachers tell it, I always stood out in the class. Whether it was doing arts and crafts, or rehearsing for the school play, I just wanted to make my parents proud of me. The times I remember and enjoyed the most were the times after school because I got to hang out with my sister Melody.

Melody has always been and always will be a control freak. She loved taking Karina and me places. We always played this game where if she saw a cute boy she wanted to flirt with, we were little sisters;

however, if it was somebody hitting on her that she wanted to get rid of—we pretended to be her kids. It worked to perfection because she is 14 years older than me and told everyone with such conviction, that the boy always believed her.

"Hola mamacita—no quieres que sea tú papacito?"

"Move it, buddy! I'm waiting for my husband. He'll be here any minute!"

Most of the time, though, she just wanted to be my big sister.

"Kilina—what do you want to do this weekend?"

"I don't know, Melody . . . maybe go to the beach." because I know how much she always wanted to go to the beach, especially *Rosarito*.

"That sounds like a brilliant idea. I trained you well," she would say.

What I love about Melody is that she can seem like she doesn't really care, but I know deep down that she cares a lot. One example is when we went camping and she talked to me about careers:

"Kilina—what do you want to be when you grow up?"

"I don't know . . . sometimes, I think I would like to be a veterinarian, but I really don't get biology that well. Other times, I think I would like to go into business for myself—but, then, I remember all of the jobs that I've had. I really don't want to devote all of my time and energy to a business!"

"What is your passion?" she asked me.

"I don't know if it's my passion, but helping other people with their problems. I don't mean fixing their mistakes. It's more of listening to what they have to say—and letting them figure out what they need to do to solve their own problems."

"Maybe you should be a psychiatrist?"

"How's that working for you?" We both laughed at the implication because Melody studied to be a psychologist.

"You know what you need to do. There is a test that you can take at the university that will give you some ideas on what you would be good at. It's called the Motivational Appraisal of Personal Potential, or MAPP. I think you should sign up for it," she told me.

The following week, I took the test and the results said: "You would do very well in the area of clinical psychology."

"Melody, I know what I want to be when I grow up?"

"What's that?"

"I want to be your little sister!"

I consider Fernando my brother too—even though he's technically my brother-in-law since he's married to Melody. He's a fire inspector for the City of Chula Vista. I love him because he's a big *alcahuete* and he's always there when I need a friend, or a big brother. One thing he said to me recently that stands out in my mind is he asked: "If your house was burning down, and you could only save one thing, what would you save and why?"

I had to think about this a little bit, but I knew immediately afterwards what to say: "I would save all my pictures because they are irreplaceable."

"What makes your pictures irreplaceable?" Fernando asked.

"Well, for one thing, they're a memory of everything that has happened so far in my life. Like the pictures I have of being on the beach at your wedding—those are really special. If I didn't have those pictures, I probably wouldn't remember all of the details of what happened there."

"Kilina . . . I feel so special to be a part of your family."

"I love you too, Fernando!"

With my biological brother, Stevan—it's a whole different relationship. *Por la buena es bien bueno conmigo*—but, I better not get on his bad side. One time I asked him if he could help me find a job.

"What kind of a job are you looking for, babe?" he asked.

"I really don't know, but something that pays more than minimum wage," I told him.

The very next day, he told me to call his boss and, within a week, I was working for Migrant Glass at $10.00 an hour as a receptionist. Wow! That was really cool.

Another time, some friends brought me home and they wanted me to go to the movies with them. I went into the house to see if my dad was home, but only my brother was there. So I went back outside to tell my friends, and they were in no hurry, so we started talking again. A little bit later, Steve came out and told me to get inside the house. I really didn't take him serious because he had never acted jealous or protective with me before. I just ignored him. When he came out the second time, he was pissed:

"**Kilina**—I told you to get back inside the house!"

"I'm coming—hold your horses!"

"I already warned you, I want you inside, **NOW!**"

"I'll come inside when I'm ready!"

That was obviously the wrong choice of words for him. He came out to where I was leaning against my friend's car and grabbed me by the hair. He literally dragged me inside of the house. Then he went back outside the house and chased my friends away. *Estaba endemoniado!* I had never seen him that way before and we stopped talking to each other for a month after that. The worst part was yet to come though. When my dad got home, both my mom and Melody corralled him and told him that if he didn't tell Steve to move out of the house, they were going to get a restraining order and have the police come and pick him up. My dad, against his better judgment, told Steve that he had to move out—and the consequences if he didn't go. Steve got his little *chivas* together and moved out that night.

I don't remember him apologizing to me, or me to him because it's always kind of understood between siblings that we're not the enemy. We are going to have some rough patches because we try to emulate our parents once in a while, but that's never our domain. The only thing we can definitely do to iron out these rough spots is to love one another unconditionally because that's what brothers and sisters are supposed to do.

CHAPTER 10

KARINA

ALL CHILDREN are unique and special, but Karina falls into an extra-special category and not just because she is my sibling. You see she was born with a cerebellar astrocytoma, which is a fancy way of saying she had a star-shaped tumor wrapped around the brain stem. The way my dad would describe it was like a fist grabbing at her spinal cord. When the doctors first went in to operate, they removed the palm of the hand first. However, she still needed three more surgeries to remove the fingers. The problem was that they were wrapped so tight that the surgeons took part of the brain stem with it.

When Karina was born, she walked with a gait and she spoke a little funny—like she was a *chiqueada*. Nobody really paid much attention until Guyo, my maternal grandmother, said: *"Algo anda mal con esa niña!"* or "Something is wrong with that little girl!" It wasn't until she started running a fever of one hundred and three with hot and cold chills that my parents decided to take her to a pediatrician, Dr. Cindy Fugii, who diagnosed the tumor. After the neurosurgeon at Kaiser, Dr. Susan Paré, performed the operation, she told my parents she had done all she could do for Karina. Around the same time, my parents read an article in <u>Reader's Digest</u> regarding Dr. Fred Epstein who had performed dozens of these operations with miraculous results. My parents phoned the doctor. He told them to send him her MRI/CT scans. Within a week's time, he phoned my parents and told them if they could get Karina to New York, he would perform the operation she needed to remove the rest of the tumor. When my parents found this out, they scheduled an audience with the surgeons at Kaiser who, in turn, sent them to Dr. Hector James, a neurosurgeon at Rady's Children's Hospital in San Diego. The rest is history because my sister is alive and cancer free today.

During the years Karina was in and out of the hospital, my sister Melody took care of me. These were good times because I got to hang out with teenagers who were 12-14 years older than me. I was the official team mascot. The only challenge was when Karina came home from the hospital; I was expected to do everything for her.

"**Karina!** Pick up your clothes off the bathroom floor!" I yelled.

"Kilina—don't yell Just ask her to do it nicely. Remember *el tonito*. Your tone of voice makes a difference," my mom would say.

I remember going to the movies with Karina and she asked me, "Kilina—do you want any more popcorn?" When I told her, "Not right now!" She proceeded to pick the kernels of popcorn off the theater floor and put it into our bucket.

"**Karina!** What the heck do you think you're doing?"

"You said you didn't want any more," Karina explained.

"I said **'Not right now!'** You just ruined a perfectly good bucket of popcorn."

"I didn't want to leave a mess on the floor because you would yell at me."

"Now she decides to pickup after herself," I thought out loud.

Another time I was feeling generous, so I took Karina to get a manicure and pedicure at the nail salon on a Saturday. I made the mistake of asking her if she wanted acrylic nails.

"What are 'crylic' nails?" she asked.

"They are fake nails that look really nice," I told her.

"Okay! I want some then," she said.

They came out looking really nice and natural. I felt proud of myself for treating her. There was only one major problem. The 'crylic' nails lasted less than a week. On Monday, she put stripper on them and painted them over with Hanna Montana glitter polish. By Wednesday, she was biting the polish off; then she decided they needed trimming, so she cut them down to the quick. By Friday, we were back in the nail salon getting the 'crylic' nails removed. My mom still hasn't let me live that one down.

Karina can be fun to be with too. One time when my family was going on vacation, Karina convinced my dad that they would probably need a disposable underwater camera for the waterfall in Jamaica. The only problem was we weren't going anywhere near Jamaica, but my dad bought her the camera any way. On a sunny day, we got off the ship at Key West, Florida. My dad found a mini-tram that was supposed to take us on a 70-minute tour of the city for $35.00. When we got on the train, my mom wanted to sit in the very front car and my dad sat underneath the canopy. As soon as everyone got situated, the tour guide told us: "Let me pass out these plastic ponchos—just in case we have a cloudburst."

No sooner did he finish with his warning than here came the rain. At first, it was no more than a sprinkle; but, sooner than later, it became a torrential downpour. Every time the train stopped at some landmark on the tour that we couldn't see because of the tropical storm, the water that had accumulated on the canopy fell directly on my dad. Karina was quick to point out: "See dad—this is the perfect opportunity to use the underwater camera!"

My sister, the comedian. You know it's hard to live with her, but I really don't know what I would do without her. She makes me livid sometimes—and, sometimes, she makes me want to cry. She can make me laugh until my stomach hurts from all of the craziness. And, you know what? I wouldn't want anyone else in the world for my sister because I love her very much.

CHAPTER 11
CONVERSATIONS AT THE DINNER TABLE

ONE OF THE FUN THINGS about eating at our house is the conversation at the dinner table. The Velas don't eat dinner together every day; but, when we do, it's always magnanimous. Like the time Melody asked for everyone to pick one person to say something nice about and to go around the table and share their thoughts. Melody started off: "I want to tell you Kilina that I appreciate everything you do because you do it with a smile and you make me laugh—even when I feel like crying sometimes."

Fernando's turn was next: "I want to tell you that I'm so proud of being part of your family because from day one, you've made me feel like I belong and because you seem to know the right thing to say whenever you start a conversation."

Karina spoke next: "Kilina, I just wanted to tell you that you make me so happy when you come home and you sleep in my bed because you're warm blooded—not like mom who has cold feet—and you make me feel loved and needed."

During Stevan's time, he got sentimental: "I also want to tell you how proud I am that you are my sister. I never thought that having a sister that was 12 years younger than me could make a difference, but you have. You make me appreciate everything you say because you say it from the heart—and Malú loves you too because you made her feel like one of the family on the day we got engaged."

Malú jumped in: "¡Sí es cierto! You are one of a kind. You're loving and considerate of everyone, especially people who are new to your family—hint, hint—and you made me feel like having a daughter who will grow up just like you."

I gestured, "Thank you, Malú."

My mom said it best: "*Eres muy especial!* You're the one who most reminds me of your father because you look like him—without the mustache of course; and you act like him in so many ways, like when you speak, you don't just speak your mind. You listen to what everyone else has to say; then you give your opinion, which is always direct and to the point. You are definitely wise beyond your years."

Then it was Kilina's turn to speak:

"Melody . . . I love you because—not only are you my sister, but you're also my best friend—and I don't know what I would do without you."

"Fernando . . . you're so special to me because you're always there when I need you and I love you like my brother."

"Stevan . . . I know we have our differences of opinion at times, but you'll always be my big brother—no matter what you do—and I love you, too."

"Malú . . . you're like my real sister. I don't know you as well as Melody, but I want to get to know you better—and when you have a daughter, I have a few things I want her to know about handling her dad."

"Karina . . . I like sleeping with you, too—except you keep stealing all of the covers. You're a very spoiled child. I know because it takes one to know one."

"Mom . . . I know we fight a lot and we seemed to disagree on almost everything, but I'm glad you are my mom because you are strong, and I know I can always come to you with my problems. I know if I make a decision, you'll respect it and that means a lot to me. I love you mom . . ." I paused a moment and then I spoke with conviction: "Dad—if you are listening to this, don't think for one minute that I've forgotten about you. You're still the glue that holds this family together!"

Everyone in the family chimed in, *"Que asi sea!"*

MEMORIES OF MY FATHER

WHILE AT CSULB, I took a Child Literature 104 class where they gave me the assignment of writing about my dad. Initially, all I could think about was that I wanted to interview my dad because he would know what to write about, but I remembered that my dad had taught me that the easiest way to overcome writer's block was to sit down and begin to write. He swore that even if you wrote the same ideas over and over again—eventually, you would instinctively know what to write next. After several futile attempts and several rewrites, I wrote the following:

My dad's name was Estevan with a V instead of a B because his parents wanted him to be one of a kind. Gabriel Garcia Marquez wrote a short story "The Handsomest Drowned Man" about a town that adopts a castaway because he represented something that they didn't have, mainly a hero. They named the man Esteban because, according to Greek mythology, he was their god of fertility. When I researched that name, I found out that Esteban was the first martyr of the Catholic Church who was stoned to death for teaching about Christ. Apparently, Marquez's fascination with the name had more to do with him being a loner. The name Vela is also curious because in English, the word means candle and my dad was definitely a lot like that.

My dad did not wear jewelry or any expensive accessories, he was an extremely simple person and anyone who met him would notice his simplicity. But, for as long as I can remember my dad carried a black pen in his shirt pocket, a comb in his back pocket, and he just couldn't seem to get rid of an old blue and white Spartan polo shirt. The Spartans were the Chula Vista High School's mascot where my dad taught and I graduated from as a student. These three items scream Estevan Vela—my dad.

Throughout my life, there have been hundreds of replacements for the black ballpoint pens, but they were always the same make and model. I think this writing utensil showed my dad's characteristic of being so organized. You see my dad loved to have everything neat and orderly, which was exemplified through his penmanship—every letter had to be exactly the same height and width. Consequently, when he was in need of a pen to write down his thoughts or feelings, he knew exactly where to look in his shirt pocket near to his heart.

The second item, his comb, was always in his right hand back pocket, but it's not any less important. I believe the comb represented my dad's tendency to be vain. He was not a conceited man, but I do think he was a very well groomed one. The comb simply allowed him to slick back his hair at any given time. He hated for his hair to get wavy in back, so the comb prevented it from looking sloppy. He had every hair in its place and a place for every hair.

The third item, the Spartan polo shirt completes the simple paradox that was my dad. First of all, it contradicted his vanity because the old shirt was worn so often, it had holes in it. I think the shirt showed how important it was to my dad to be loyal. You see, sometimes school was the last place my dad wanted to be, but he never called in sick and he never complained; even though he was passed over several times for promotions he felt he had earned at the school. He dreamed about being the baseball coach for many years, but every time the position opened up, they always passed my dad over to give it to someone else. He worked tirelessly and always put in more energy than was needed. You see 'giving it his all' was his trademark. It was how he handled every situation. The good thing about this was my dad wasn't just loyal to his school; he was loyal to his family and to his friends as well—even when the loyalty wasn't reciprocated.

Although these three items are distinct in many ways, they represent the consistency and continuity that was my dad. On the flip side, when my dad liked something, he was resentful to change. That's just the way he was. There are many reasons for people to become teachers, but few people become teachers to learn how to become a better person like my dad.

CHAPTER 13

BETTER THAN NOTHING

SOME UNSTABLE PERSON said there was always something to write about. I beg to differ. This is an assignment for my Lit. 104 Class that is everything you always wanted to know about nothing.

To begin with, my Nany used to make us a dessert called 'Better than Sex'; however, my grandparents were a little bit prudish, so they decided to call it 'Better than Nothing' because that was a favorite saying of my grandfather, so I decided to use it for this assignment.

So, in keeping with this theme, here are some of my thoughts . . . whoever thought of the idea that there had to be twenty-four hours in a day. Yeah, I know, 365 rotations of the Earth around the sun—yara, yara, and yara. Why couldn't it have been 12 hours a day of 120 minutes per hour? And, while we are on the subject—why do we have breakfast, lunch and dinner? Why couldn't we have one big meal in the middle of the day and call it blinner, or a lot of snacks in between? (It works for most animals.) I have been listening to two songs; one by John Lennon called 'Imagine', and a *rock en español* group named *Sin Banderas*. It occurs to me that this whole idea of having so many countries (Did you see the march of nations at the Olympics?) has got to go. Why? Simply because we have the technology, the resources and the people to do almost anything that's humanly conceivable, but we choose to segregate ourselves and make the world a better place for a few and a miserable place for many. On the subject of global warming for example, we have the wherewithal to make cars that use biodegradable fuel or hydrogen; however, we are still dependent on fossil fuels because there are huge lobbies by the oil industry to keep it that way. Who says it has to be that way? Oh, I get it—that's the way the World Bank is set up. Well—guess what? Why not redistribute the wealth so that everybody has enough to eat and no children starve to death? We don't have to do away with capitalism; I think the people who work the hardest should make the most money. When I think about how we distribute the natural resources now, it's shameful. Think about it! A celebrity commits a crime, and then s/he goes on probation. When s/he breaks the rules of said probation, s/he gets to pay a fine and do more probation. Where is the justice in that?

On the subject of religion . . . I believe that Jesus is the Son of God, but weren't Moses, Abraham, Isaac and Joseph also sons of the same God? Obviously, we give Jesus special treatment because he suffered greatly and he was resurrected. If this is the case why do we have so many Christian sects if it's the same Jesus? Why are non-Christian religions less important? If God wanted everybody to be saved through Christianity, how come two thirds of the world's population is Chinese? Somehow, some way aren't Mohammed, Buddha, Vishnu and the Virgin Mary all related? What about the six degrees of separation? I know, I know—somebody out there is going to say that these are just the crazy musings of a college student that doesn't have anything else to do with her time, that my time would be better spent watching repeats of "Sex in the City" or "Law and Order." But, you know what? My ideas didn't just occur to me out of the blue. They are a genuine product of nineteen years of education and acculturation, so why can't I be the catalyst to change things.

While we are on the topic of television . . . I propose to watch half as much television as I did last year; therefore, I will watch TV with one eye closed. Now, answer me this: Why is it that there are 200 channels on the cable network, but 75 are devoted to infomercials, 35 to reruns of old shows, 25 devoted to world and local NEWS, 15 are

BETTER THAN NOTHING

devoted to Christian evangelists; another 15 devoted to soap operas that never seem to end. At least ten devoted to sports I've never heard of. The channels that are left—I have little or no interest in watching. It's almost as bad at the movies because, if I really want to see a movie bad enough, I can spend $20.00 on gas to get to the movie; $10.50 for a ticket to get into the show; $15.00 for a popcorn, a soda and a bag of M&M's; or, I can wait for three months and watch the movie in the comfort of my living room for $3.00 rental on DVD. What's up with that?

What about using common sense? My dad taught me something he called the Antonio paradox. You see Antonio worked for my grandfather as a handyman who was forced into being a hunting guide when there was no one else to do it. The contradiction came when Mr. Hulahand, a long time duck hunter, told my grandfather, *"Antonio es muy buen hombre—no sabe ganso!"* or "Antonio is a very good man—he doesn't understand geese!" According to my dad's version of the story, every duck hunter knows that you should always build your duck blind upwind. There are two distinct but very important purposes. First of all, when you scare up the geese, they will fly with the wind to the next station. Secondly, geese will not be able to pick up the human scent if the wind is blowing toward you. The only time a duck can smell you is when the wind is blowing against you in their direction.

Antonio's flaw was he used to drive his motorboat into the flock of birds ensuring the birds would scatter and essentially come back and land in the same place. However, common sense would dictate, when the birds cannot hear, smell and see you coming from downwind, they will expediently vacate their position and fly upwind to the next station where the duck blind is located. The reason for this analogy is especially poignant because it's just common sense; and that's what few of our politicians want us to use these days.

On the subject of fashion design, who said that green shoes don't go with a purple dress? Or that pomegranate doesn't match my skin tone? One of the things that I learned from my dad was that almost everything goes well with blue denim. I wear my Levi's jacket to class, to church, to Kariff's soccer game, to a wedding, a 50ᵗʰ wedding anniversary, a Shakespearean play, a birthday party, or just to keep my shoulders warm on a chilly night—it doesn't matter as long as I feel comfortable wearing it.

Finally, I want to address the issues of my parents always being right. Who died and made them the experts? There is no course in any institution of higher learning that I know of called Parenting 101, so where do parents get off telling us the best solution to every problem? I mean half the time that I ask my mom for permission to do some thing, she already has a reason for me not to do it. So what's the purpose of asking permission? I remember hearing my dad say, "It's better to ask forgiveness than it is to ask for permission." When I ask my mom for her blessing to stay at Ana's house, she always says "No!" but, if I just go there directly from Long Beach—instead of coming home, she never says anything about it. So, it must be that asking for permission is the wrong thing to do, although my mom would never admit to that. Go figure?

THE PROBLEM WITH MY MOM

I THINK PART OF THE PROBLEM with my mom is that she was never actually allowed to be a kid. For example, she likes to tell everyone who will listen that she was a hippy, and that she walked barefoot on the streets of Tijuana. However, she never did any kind of drugs; she never hitchhiked or went anywhere on a road trip. She lived in a convent for Pete's sake. She didn't sleep with my dad before they got married—even though many people in her family thought they did. And, she never lied to her mother; apparently, because that's what she claims to be the most proud of. Well, I think that the truth can be as dangerous as a lie if it's used for the wrong reason.

My mom was always getting into trouble with her mom, her family and her friends because she insisted on telling them the truth—even when they didn't want to hear it. I remember her having a fight with my dad because she criticized his driving. My dad was not a pride-driven person, but he did take a lot of pride in his driving. My mom's contention was that he had somehow lost his ability to drive carefully because he would either signal at the last moment, or perhaps—not at all—before making a lane change. To which my mom would always say, "I don't know what's happening to you, but you're losing it, guy!" That was a real insult to my dad because he claimed that he never made a maneuver unless he saw in his rearview and side mirrors that he was clear to do so. My mom's rebuttal was that he was just making excuses to try to cover up for a bad decision; however, my dad argued that he had never caused an accident because of poor driving or lack of judgment. My mom replied, "That's not true because the reason I have this scar on my head is that you made the wrong judgment and fell asleep the wheel!" Once again, this was a true statement. My dad did fall asleep while driving to Las Vegas to do a job for the soils testing company that he worked for back in the 70ties. He claimed that it wasn't his fault because he had called his boss, Dan Goodwin, to tell him that he needed to get a few hours sleep. Dan told him that it would be better for him to get on the road because Las Vegas was at least six hours from San Diego and my dad needed to be there by 6:00 AM in the morning.

My dad and mom started from San Diego at 10:00 PM at night. When they reached Hesperia, my dad woke my mom up to tell her that this was where they had purchased a lot earlier in the year. After that, he said he didn't remember anything—except for the screeching metal and breaking glass on the truck. When the truck stopped skidding on the pavement, my dad crawled out the side window. He saw the truck turned upside down and my mom trapped inside. They had to use the jaws-of-life to get my mother out of the wreckage. My mom spent 11 days in the intensive care unit, and three more years in therapy because of that accident. So she had every right to be pissed off at my dad, but it's just one example of how the truth can often be more cruel than accepting that some accidents can't be avoided, so the perpetrators need to be exonerated of the blame.

Another problem with my mom is that she has this warped sense of righteousness because she feels that she is closer to God, so she must be right! I think that is just wrong. My grandmother, Nany, wasn't close to God, but she acted more Christian toward everyone than my mom does. Somebody once said, "forgiveness is divine." My mom can't be right all the time because she holds grudges and doesn't forget anything that someone does to her—I don't think that's very Christ like at all.

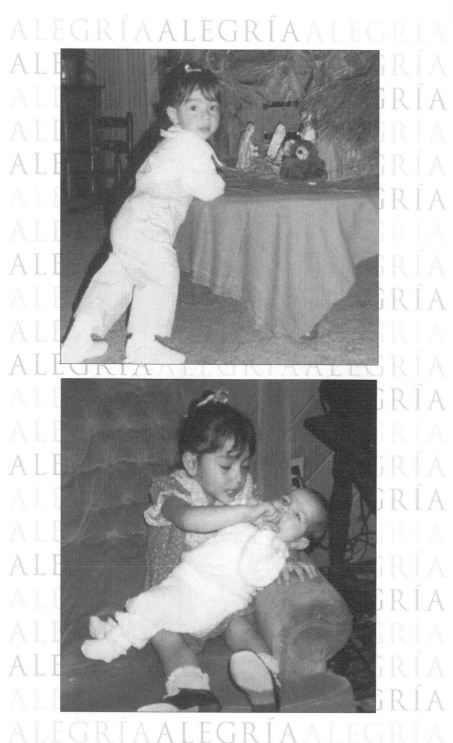

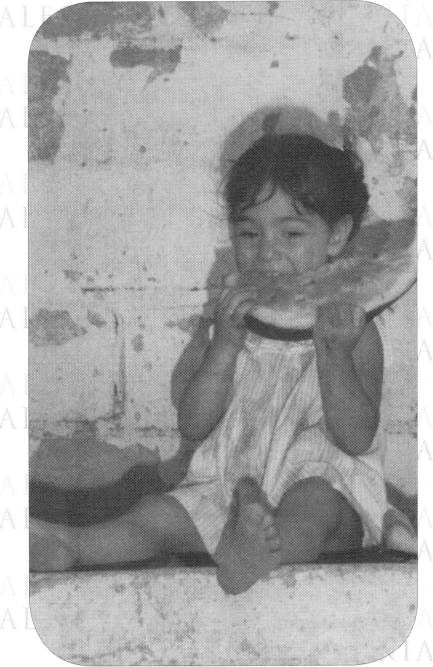

My mom tells the story of how she was once implicated in a rumor when her relatives blamed her for losing a letter that a boyfriend had sent her Cousin *Mayita*. It was a family dispute, but my mom was smack dab in the middle. My *Nina Vita*, her dad's sister asked her straight out, "Did you lose the letter?" My mom said, "Absolutely not!" So *Nina Vita* said, "Can you swear on the Holy Bible that you didn't lose the letter?" My mom said "Yes!" so *Nina Vita*, who was basically the enforcer in the *Magaña* family, took her before the sacristy to tell God and the rest of the family that she didn't lose the letter. Later on, she found out her Uncle *Marco* had the letter and was keeping it to test her. My mom told me she swore that she had nothing to do with it and hadn't even seen the letter, but she never forgot it and she reminded everyone at her *Nina's* funeral what she made her do.

Having told this story, the exception would be if someone in her immediate biological family did something wrong, then she's the first one to ask that they be forgiven, like the time that her father tried to molest my cousin when she was a little girl. My mom somehow found justification in it because he was an old man—and he really didn't know what he was doing. The problem was that her father had been doing this most of his adult life with all kinds of girls and women— and he had children with several women outside of wedlock. The tall and the short of it was that my grandfather was a pedophile, and he got away with it thanks to my mom and other members of his family who never held him accountable. Melody still hasn't forgiven my mom for that one.

This brings me to an argument I am having with my mom right now. I told her that she goes too far when someone tells her "No!" She claims that she won't accept "No!" for an answer if it's not what she believes in. The other day, my brother Stevan was taking Malú for a quiet weekend out, so they asked Dora, a friend of the family, to stay with Alessandra, their new born daughter. They told my mom, "Please feel free to drop by and make sure the baby is all right." My mom interpreted this as, "Feel free to come by and take the baby out any time." So my mom came to see Dora the next day to tell her she was going to take them to Sunday mass. It wasn't just any mass. It was my Cousin Emilio's *Cantamisa* (all 4 1/2 hours worth.) The conversation went something like this:

"Dora—voy a venir por la niña como las 9:30 de la mañana. I'm coming to get you and the baby at 9:30 in the morning."

"Gracias. I don't feel comfortable taking the baby outside yet!" Dora replied.

"Don't worry. I'll help you take care of the baby."

"I'm not worried, but I'm not ready to take the baby anywhere— least of all to a church where I don't know anyone."

"If you're worried about my son and daughter-in-law, they won't say anything because they know you and I will take good care of the baby."

"You're not listening to the words coming out of my mouth—I'm not taking the baby out because I don't think it's the right thing to do!" Dora told her emphatically.

"Oh, but I understand—you don't feel confident enough, but I do! I know everyone that's going to be at the ceremony and it will be okay because we are just going to church and . . ."

Okay, you get the idea. It's like two people talking where neither one is listening to what the other person is saying. Finally, my brother had to call my mom and politely tell her to back off; otherwise, Dora promised she would never babysit for them again.

So, my mom never got to be a kid because she was too busy dealing with all of these adult issues and being responsible for things kids shouldn't have to deal with. That's why she acts like a child most of the time now. Maybe it's not her fault, but it would be nice if she acknowledged this is why she is the way she is now. The bottom line is that my mom is not perfect—no person is, but I love her anyway.

CHAPTER 15

PERIBAN

LAST YEAR AT THIS TIME, my mom decided to take my grandmother, *Guyo Chiquito,* to *Periban, Michoacan* during Easter Break. This was both a Mother's Day present and a way for my mom and her sisters to get back in touch with their heritage and their mother's roots. It happened during my spring break, so I really didn't have any excuse not to go; besides, my mom offered to pay my way so I figured I needed a vacation: "What the heck!"

It was kind of a funny trip because we got a ride to the airport with my dad's friend from school, Benita. Her car had a major break down, but she got us to the airport. This should have been an omen for us, but we chose to ignore it. We hopped on board a jet plane and traveled three hours to *Morelia, Michoacan,* which is one of the most beautiful cities in *México.* The architecture is from the fifteenth century, but its streets are colorful and noisy because it's a college Mecca. *Morelia* is home to one of the most progressive universities in all of *México,* so there is a ton of students who come here from places near and far.

From there, we got on a very modern bus that had all the amenities and traveled about an hour to *Uruapan*—not like *Morelia,* but a fairly large bustling city. This place is most famous for making *carnitas,* which is a deep fried pork dish. From *Uruapan,* we got on an urban bus where somebody selling something gets on at every stop, and they fill up the bus to the point that it gets hard to breath inside. They sell candy, *buñuelos, chicles, cajeta*, homeopathic medicine and tealeaves that can cure anything—including dementia. You need something like this before you decide to get on this bus. This was a two-hour ride that lasted an eternity. Finally, we got off the bus and spent another 45 minutes trying to hail a cab that could take all nine of us and our luggage to *Tia Amparo's* house in the middle of *Periban*. We ended up walking for another half-hour.

When we finally got there, we spent another 45 minutes hugging, kissing and getting to know 93-year-old *Tia Amparo* who was deaf and half-senile, and *Martita* who takes care of her. They live in a house that was built around 150 years ago—very similar to how *Frida Kahlo* described her home in her autobiography. It was in the shape of a big horseshoe. In the middle of the edifice, there is a *soler*, which is a type of garden with several kinds of fruit trees. One side of the horseshoe had a balcony where you could look down on the garden from upstairs bedrooms; however, the rest of the house just had an overhang that helped protect you from the water that poured down from the roof during a rainstorm that would come later on the trip. For the next ten days, this was both our sanctuary and our prison because we ate, slept and prayed there morning, noon and night.

The real story of this home lies on a small plaque on the wall of the music room next to the letters and newspaper articles of the matriarch of the family. It was dedicated to *Baldina 'Nina' Aviña* for 50 years of outstanding service to the *niños* of *Periban*. You see Nina, as everyone called her, was a pre-school teacher before this community even understood the concept of Head Start. She didn't have a conventional classroom, but she took 20 to 30 children at a time and taught them life skills. Most days they sat on fruit crates in front of an old slate chalkboard. She taught them how to be neat and courteous—even refined. The morning was dedicated to learning to read and write; midday to math and a little bit of science, like how to plant a seed and make it grow. The afternoons were dedicated to learning music.

Nina taught them their first letters and numbers. Somehow she breathed curiosity into them so they took her words home like precious stones to use again and again over their lifetime. She taught them hygiene by comparing cleanliness to godliness, so they felt embarrassed to show up the next day with dirt under their fingernails. Finally, she taught them to appreciate music by playing the piano and the violin for them so they could understand about compassion and empathy for one another. She taught them a new hunger, a new attitude and a new direction. Above all she taught them to live their lives well.

The reason for making this trip, besides giving Guyo a Mother's Day present, was to attend Cousin Mari's wedding. On that day, we got to dress in our Sunday best and go to 11:00 AM mass for the ceremony. What was strange and inspiring at the same time was how our 93-year-old great Tia Amparo slowly made her way to the front of the church. She wanted the rest of the family to recognize her, and for the priest to give her communion first—as if the wedding ritual was an afterthought.

"Muevete, move over!" she said, *"Necesito que el padre me vea."*

It's kind of peculiar that the comic genius George Allen said, "Youth is wasted on the young!" because, in *México,* the old people take precedence over the young. That's not to say that they are undeserving, or that they should be ignored; it's just that, in a weird funny sort of way, the young are not expected to outshine their predecessors. This fascinates me because I think this is the reason that the United States has lost its majestic status and is out of touch with the rest of the world. In the U.S. we simply have written off our elderly. We live in a culture where being old is kind of a handicap and staying young is an obsession.

"Es un placer tenerlos aquí en nuestra boda—it's a pleasure to have you here at our wedding," Mari told us.

"It's an honor and a privilege for us to be here," I answered.

"*Ojalá se puedan quedar unos dias*—I hope you are planning to stay for a few days," she added.

"*Pensamos estar de perdida una semana*—we'll be here for at least another week," I nodded in agreement.

"*Entonces que se diviertan y bailen mucho*—Have fun and dance a lot," Cousin Mari encouraged to us.

"*Eso pensamos hacer*—We plan to do just that," I motioned with my index finger.

We partied until we couldn't party anymore. My *Tio Ramon* got drunk as a skunk, and my mom warned me not to get too interested in the boys at the party because they were probably my cousins.

The next few days were both frantic and boring. We spent most of the morning planning what we wanted to do. Then, the rest of the day was carrying out the plan, like the day we went to *el Parque Nacional de Uruapan* or *Cupatitzio*. It was a fairly innocent proposal to go there; however, once we were there, the brother and sisters insisted on renting wheelchairs—even though there were no ramps or wheelchair access. That meant that we had to carry the wheelchairs with the *Tia* down 28 crumbling stairs and back up again. It was sheer misery. We pulled and pulled and grunted while lifting the chair over the rocky bumps that made the stairway—even though we rested in between. I used muscles and ligaments I had never used before, or plan to use any time in the immediate future.

This would have been torture enough; nevertheless, this was not the end of day. About four o'clock in the afternoon, we exited the park and drove around looking for a place to eat. After an hour or so, the five leaders decided that we should go to *Paracho*, which was two hours away. Add to these 30 minutes trying to find a bathroom for Karina. By the time we finally found a place to park next to the restaurant, everyone voted that I stay with *Tia Amparo,* and they would bring us something to eat. I wasn't even famished anymore because my anger stifled my hunger. When we got home that night, I felt like death warmed over several times. I didn't even have enough energy to brush my teeth. I collapsed in a heap of dust that was my bed and fell into a deep sleep.

What I'll remember most about *Periban* is what my *Tia Elvirita* said when we first got there, *"Este es un pueblo bicicletero,"* which loosely translated means, *"This is a one bicycle town."*

CHAPTER 16

P2

ONE OF THE ANOMALIES that doesn't get mentioned in our family is the fact that on my *Guyo's* side of the family, we are *Aviñas*. The reason that this is different is because the *Magañas* are also *Aviñas* on their mother's side. My grandparents were actually first cousins. When they got married, there was a big scandal—so much so, that they were not allowed to live close to the rest of the family. For their first year, they actually lived in a stable when they came to *Maneadero, Baja California.* Some of my *tios* actually supported them behind everyone's back. This is a story for another time and not the fun part I want to address here.

Whenever the *Aviñas* get together, there is sure to be a party to follow. Like when we were in *Periban,* we went to the wedding where everything was colorful and elegant. However, the *tornoboda* that happened at my *Tio Valdito's* ranch the next day was the real party. My *tio* had one of his friends make us *carnitas.* However no *carnitas* are ever complete without the fixings: *frijoles charros, arroz con mole, buché, chicharrones, cueritos, guacamole, queso fresco* and lots of *salsa* (medium hot, hot and nuclear.) And what would a *Mexican* party be without *cerveza and tequila?* The catch is that the *Aviñas* don't really drink *tequila,* it's more like *aguardiente,* which literally means 'firewater.'

The conversation usually centers on the guests: Who's invited and doesn't show up; and who was not invited, but showed up anyway. The fun part is when something happens out of the blue, like the groom's mom falling down the steps. My *Tio Valdito* was quick to point out: *"Tiene problemas renales!" Porque? Porque está re-nalgona!"* Translating this makes it less humorous, but the lady fell down because her backside was too large. Someone else at the party called her *Nico* , or *"Ni con que tirarse un pedo!"* This is the epicenter of what makes the Aviñas fun to be around. You have to be careful what you say and do because one of your relatives will make fun of you.

Now, it doesn't matter what the topic is: It could be politics or religion, or global warming. With so much food and drink around, sooner than later, the topic is flatulence. If you eat too much, you're a *'pedorra'*. If you don't eat enough, you're a *'peditos'*. If you drink too much, you're *'pedo bien contento'*. *If you're an old fart, you're 'Don Pedotes'*. If your constipated or you're just plain stupid, you're a *'tapado'*. If you're disgusted about talking about this subject, *'traes un pedo atorado'* (you're unable to fart.) If you're conceited, you're a *'pedante'*. The list goes on and on, but you better not pass some gas and try to blame it on someone else, and then get caught because you become *'el pedorro'*, or *'la pedorra'*.

While we were sitting at the table, my *tio* abruptly asked: *"Quien se echo una?"* Who farted? Everyone looked around, but no one wanted to admit anything because they knew what their punishment would be. I knew it was my duty to own up to the truth.

"Yo fuí, Tio!" I told him.

"Ay, Mi'ja –ahora si que eres de la familia! Now I know you belong to the family."

I even took the time to translate my tio's poem about this indiscretion:

> *Somebody once asked me,*
> *'What is a pedo?'*
> *I answered quite softly,*

A pedo is a pedo!'
Its skeleton made of air, its body of wind.
A pedo is like a tortured soul,
Sometimes it blows, sometimes it pops,
No matter how much you try, you can't make it stop.
A pedo is like a cloud that inconspicuously flies.
It fumigates and torments everyone as it goes by.
It has something that always entertains us.
Sometimes it sighs and sometimes it cries.
Sometimes it makes you wipe tears from your eyes.
A pedo is air and a pedo is noise—
Sometimes it even takes us by surprise.
Some pedos are strong, some are a trip—
Because every once in a while, we all let one rip!
In this world, a pedo represents hope—
Everyone has one, even the Pope.
There are cultured ones and ignorant ones.
There are adult and even infant ones.
Some are fat and some are thin,
Some make you mad, and some make you grin.
It doesn't matter if you're free of lactose,
What really matters is the size of the tacos!
If some day a pedo knocks at your door,
Don't try to stop it—just let it roar, let it pop
Cause nothing in the world can make it stop!

The *Aviñas* have so much fun with this that they even have nick-names for their relatives, like my *Tio Pedro* becomes *'Pedocles'. Tio Felipe* becomes *'Felipedo'. Tio Valdo* becomes *Tio Maldito—por pe-dorro*! Me . . . they call me Kili-nice. Psssst.

CHAPTER 17
THE REAL DEAL

LAST NIGHT I had a dream that was very much like an epiphany. I dreamed that I could be anything I wanted to be—even a high school principal. That's definitely NEWS because I remember distinctly telling my dad that the last thing I wanted to be was a teacher, and you have to be a teacher before you can become the principal. The most interesting part of the dream was that I was in my office at school when the secretary came in and announced that we would be visited by the fire marshal, who would come in during our assembly to find out if we met the fire code. I remember succinctly telling her, "I won't be told by anyone what I can or cannot do at MY school!" Wow! MY school! The last time I referred to a place as my school, I was in elementary.

While I was in high school, I really didn't think about it. I had two jobs outside of school. I worked for the same Migrant Glass Company as my brother on weekdays and holidays. Also, on the weekends, I worked for Ammonite Jewelry in the evenings. Funny how, back then, school was an afterthought. The main reason I applied to the university was so I wouldn't disappoint my family, especially my dad because he worked so hard to get an education to support us. I couldn't take a break from school because it would have broken his heart.

When I graduated from high school, I told everyone who would listen that I wanted to be a dermatologist, which translates to a biomed major at college. The problem there was I wasn't a very good science student. By the end of the first semester, it was pretty obvious I needed to go back to the drawing board to figure out how I was going to reevaluate my career goal. By the end of the first semester at Cal State Long Beach, I was very homesick and sort of convinced myself to come back and take computer classes so I could get a better paying job. I was working part time at Conroy's Florist during the week after classes. I remember a conversation I had with my dad: "I need to talk with you, Dad," I told him.

"What do you want to talk about, Love?" he answered.

"You know I think it's time for me to come back home."

"You know this is your home and you can come back any time you feel like it; however, I need to warn you that the minute you cross the threshold, your whole world will be turned upside down because your mom is going to want to limit your personal freedom."

"I know that, dad—I've talked to mom about it already. It's just that I feel disconnected. Every day in Long Beach, I'm thinking about coming home and what I'm going to do on the weekends. As soon as I get home, I have to think about what I need to do once I get back to school. If I was here, at least I wouldn't have to deal with that."

Then my dad said something that was totally unexpected:

"You are exactly where you need to be to make the right decision!" Then he explained: "You don't have to make up your mind right away on where you want to be or what you want to do. You are already at the university."—Meaning that I was with a circle of friends and family that could counsel and guide me to what I wanted to do. "You don't need to go outside your comfort zone to find out what you want to be . . . " and "On the off-hand chance the you're not able to decide what you want to do with your life, you're still on the right track because I will love and support you no matter what happens."

This caught me off guard and I whined a little when I told him, "If you love and support me no matter what, why can't you love and support me if I decide to drop out of school?"

"I know you know what I mean," he told me confidently. "I'll always love and support you, but if you quit school—there is NO amount of love and support that will make you feel better about your decision. In other words, you're basing your decision on your emotion and not your common sense."

In retrospect, that was why my dad was such a good teacher. He always knew the right thing to say; otherwise, he didn't say anything at all. And, you know what? He was right—most of what I was feeling and saying were all platitudes based on how I felt. Very little, if any, had to do with common sense. One of my dad's sayings was that he didn't like missing school because he learned something from his students every day.

What is fascinating to me now, even though I can't see or touch my dad, I can still hear his voice in my ear every waking minute. I know I'm a long way from being as wise as he was, but now I know what I want to do with my life. I want to be a teacher like my dad.

CHAPTER 18
BAPTISM BY FIRE

WHEN I SAID I wanted to be a teacher, I never realized what a liberal arts education was all about. Not only do you need to be fluent in math and science, but you need to be a reading and writing teacher as well. In addition, I am taking psychology, sociology and technology in the classroom to boot. I'm not complaining—it's just an observation.

After I transferred to San Diego State, I mistakenly believed that some how my life would get less complicated, and I would have more time for my friends, but it has been just the opposite. It has been three weeks since I've seen Kariff and we've only talked casually to each other on the phone a couple of times in between.

"I know you've been busy doing homework, but I used to see a lot more when you were living in Long Beach," Kariff complained.

"Do you want some cheese with that whine?"

"It's just that you said we would have more time together once you came back home."

"Yes, I did! Although you agreed to go back to school if I came home—and I don't see you keeping your promise either," I reproached.

Kariff laughed his simpleton laugh and said, ""I couldn't go back to school just yet. With my job at Classic Car Club and my detailing business, I don't have the time . . ."

"And when were you planning to make the time?"

"The same time you plan to devote your time to keeping your promise to me," was all he said.

I still had my two jobs at Migrant and Ammonite as well as my busy school schedule. Melody had called me to apply for the *Bomberos de San Diego* scholarship the day before it was due—so that took up the rest of my spare time during the week.

What I was learning in my classes about teaching was that NO amount of schooling could prepare you for actually being a teacher on a school campus because every teacher we meet gives us the same testimonial. For example, one rule of thumb suggests that we should never scold our students openly in the classroom. It's okay to praise them collectively, but you should always reprimand them in private. I remember distinctly how my dad lit into us one day during his AVID class about not respecting each other's space. It seemed to him like we were constantly bickering and complaining about each other until—finally, he yelled at us saying, "I'm going to step outside the room until you guys and girls can put a lid on all this sense-less arguing!" When you're ready to focus yourselves on learning and paying attention to what's important, come and get me! When I come back in you had better have resolved your issues; otherwise, I'm going to transfer some people out of here to another class—and you know who you are!"

My dad was only outside for about 90 seconds MAX, but the les-son he taught us collectively was that we needed to respect each other while we were in class because, if we didn't, he wouldn't respect our position as students. Like he said, "Education is not a right; it's a privilege."

The other thing that the educational gurus say is that students do not understand sarcasm. Well, maybe that is true to a degree, but they certainly understand 'basing' on one another:

"Your momma is so dumb that you can wade through her deepest thought and not get your ankles wet!"

"Oh, yeah! Well your momma is so dumb, when you look in the

dictionary to find out the definition of dumb, they show a picture of your momma instead!"

Oh, don't get me wrong. I find educational psychology class fascinating. My teacher Ms. O'Connell told us that: *"If you walk into a room, there will always be someone who is making a fool of themselves. When you can't find that person anywhere in the room, chances are—it's you!"* The other thing I learned from my sociology teacher Stephen Jones was that: *"What a person says about you has more to do with them, the way they think and feel, than it does about you. The only way that it can affect you is if you acknowledge them. If you choose to ignore their comments, they have NO effect on you whatsoever."*

It seems to me that teaching is more about what we learn from our students than what they learn from us. Like Mrs. Hunt at Chula Vista used to say: "Students want to know how much you care before they care how much you know." There is something about this teaching gig that makes me wonder about how my dad stayed with it so long. You know he stayed in construction for ten years before he even went into the field of education. Nevertheless, once he got there, it was like a drug—he couldn't get enough of it. He spent so much time with his students, even their parents begin to question why he didn't spend more time with his family, but that didn't faze my dad in the least.

I think in the final analysis of things, you only get out of something what you are willing to put into it. That was what my father learned and that's why he was so devoted to his profession. There I go with the platitudes again; and, so I sat down and wrote a letter to my dad on my birthday:

Wednesday, June 27, 2007
Hi Dad!
It has been two years, two months, twenty-two days and eleven hours since you went away—why did you leave me? I never realized how much I depended on you for everything. Did you want to

go, or was your time on this earth over? Sometimes death seems like God's will—and, sometimes, it seems like existential bullshit! It makes me want to scream at the top of my lungs—WHY? Anything would have been preferable to your going away. I could have dealt with your being paralyzed, or even if you were here and didn't recognize who I was, but the thought of never seeing you again—EVER makes me want to choke!

Sometimes I wake up in the middle of the night and I think it has all been a bad dream, that I'll wake up and find you sleeping in your bed. Then I shake myself awake and realize, "It's not a bad dream—it's a real nightmare." You always wanted people to tell you the truth, but when mom told you the truth, you were somehow disappointed. Mom says that you're at peace now; you don't have anyone to worry about anymore, but I know different. Your spirit is screaming out to everyone who loved you: "I'm alive! It's not fair!" There are so many people who deserve to die, or need to be taken away—why you? If I could I would give an arm or a leg, or even my sight—just to have you back again. I want to know what kind of feckless creature god is to cause so much pain and suffering to good people. Dad—if you can hear me—don't forget who loves you! ;-) Kilina

THE ALPHA/BETA CULTURE

IT HAPPENED ONE DAY in Stephen Jones' sociology class. The class was playing a game called BaFa, BaFa. The class was divided into two different cultures. The premise of the group was pretty simple. The Alpha culture's objective was to be affectionate from what my home girl Olivia and I could tell. English was their primary language; they showed respect for their elders—especially the oldest male in class—Mr. Jones. Intriguingly, they talked about family instead of business and altogether, they seemed like an amenable group.

The Beta culture on the other hand was basically just opposite. Their demeanor was very serious and detached. Here the objective was all business and trading. They spoke a different language that was somehow associated with their business. For instance, if they wanted a blue card from a color-coated deck of UNO cards, the first letter of the words would begin with a B as would blue. They will ask for it by using gestures and uttering "BaFa?" If they wanted more than one card, they would just say "Bafa, Bafa?" They would repeat the utterance for the number of cards that they wanted. In the middle of this chaotic scene, Stephen Jones came up to Olivia and me to observe what we were witnessing.

"Oh my God—this is really weird," I said to Olivia. "It's like listening to aliens from another planet."

Nodding in agreement, she said: "This is really strange," I. "The people on the side that speak English are really friendly. They act funny, but they are really friendly. The people on the other side are almost antisocial, except they seem to be totally wrapped up in their trading game."

"Did they say 'Hello!' to you?" Professor Jones asked

"Not really! All they would do is hug me and they seemed to be extraordinarily affectionate toward you, Mr. Jones," Olivia mused.

"Shameless brown-nosers," I added.

The teams broke up. After that, we arranged our desks in a circle around the room, so that everyone would have equal status during the debrief. Then Stephen Jones spoke:

"Well, ladies . . . tell us what you observed from the different cultures," he said.

"First of all, this was a really bizarre experience," I explained. "Both groups came from entirely different cultures. The first group was very affectionate—almost to the point of being patronizing," I told him.

"The other group never spoke in English, which is to say they had their own code. They used utterances that we could understand—but they seemed like they were from an entirely different hemisphere," Olivia added.

"Yeah, they were more interested in trading their colored cards with one another. It was like some foreign Wall Street or something," I pointed out.

"Very good observations, ladies," Professor Jones pointed out. "Did you notice anything that made these two groups seem alike?"

"It seemed like both groups used an awful lot of hand and facial gestures to communicate—like they could have been Italians," I answered.

Olivia noted, "At least more than usual. They also both seemed oblivious to everything and everyone around them. I don't know if I'm imagining this, or is it actually happening."

"No—you weren't imagining it. Good descriptions overall . . . Now, who do you know—real people, who might experience these feelings of alienation that you spoke of ?" Jones asked.

"Immigrants." Olivia suggested.

"Eureka! How does it feel to be an alien? Professor Jones inquired.

"It feels weird, terribly strange. It feels like the people were here in body, but not in mind or spirit. I couldn't read their thoughts and they didn't seem to care about mine. I felt alone, ostracized. It wasn't a good feeling. I felt like I was pouring my heart out to try to assimilate, but they didn't care," I said.

"It felt like we were coming into a foreign country knowing that we stood out because of the way we looked and acted. I started feeling self-conscious—even inferior to the other people in this room," Olivia explained.

Suddenly, the professor turned to the rest of the class: "And how about the question of fairness?"

Roy, one of our classmates, answered: "There was NO fairness. We were the dominant culture and we knew it. We knew the rules of the game—they didn't."

"We were outfoxed and outnumbered," I conceded.

"How did it make you guys feel?" Mr. Jones asked them.

"They didn't have a clue what was going on and we were in charge from beginning to end," Roy remarked.

"Okay, now you know how it feels to be an immigrant. If you don't understand the language or the culture of the country you've immigrated to, you become disenfranchised. It's almost like being a slave. Socially, politically, economically—you are an outcast. Think about this for next time you come into contact with someone from another country .. . For next time, I want you to read Chapter 17 on the "Power of Body Language". Class dismissed!"

When the rest of the students slowly abandoned the classroom, only Olivia, Roy and I were left behind.

"I hope I didn't give you the wrong impression back there, but you look so cute when you're embarrassed," Roy chided.

"I wasn't embarrassed," I retorted

""Well, you sure did a master impression of someone who was embarrassed," Roy said mocking me.

"You know what? You are embarrassing me right now. You're annoying me and I have another class to go to. Excuse me," I feigned anger.

'I'm sorry—It wasn't my intention to annoy you. In fact, I would like to get to know you better. Do you think we might get together sometime?"

"No, I don't think so. Excuse me, but I need to get to class," I said as I pushed my way passed him.

As we walked toward the door, Olivia said beneath her breath, "Arrogant and conceited—just the way you like them!"

CHAPTER 20

WORDS

" . . . THE HOLY GOSPEL according to Luke . . .

The following Sunday, my mother, Karina and I went to church. The sermon was an interesting passage from Luke because it was about how Jesus said that he had come to "Baptize with fire"—instead of water. "To pit mother against daughter, father against son and mother-in-law against daughter-in-law." I found this fascinating because it seemed paradoxical to everything I was ever taught about Jesus—love, compassion, patience and all of that stuff. It was like trying to explain the contradiction of a quiet storm.

Father Mario, who did the homily at my dad's funeral and confused the hell out of everybody, proceeded to try to explain the meaning of fire. According to Mario, Prometheus who gave it to the humans stole fire from the gods. He explained how the 'burning bush' represented God in the Old Testament and that fire was used to cleanse that which is old and withered—it allows for new birth. He explained how the California Native Americans used to burn the sagebrush out of the forests, so that new trees could grow in the spring as a form of protecting the meadow. He told us jokingly that the U.S. Forestry Service had chastised the Indians for this ritual and allowed the forest to grow without interference, which eventually destroyed the meadowlands and interrupted the natural process in places like Yosemite. Then he turned the whole thing around and told us that fire was not always used for destructive purposes. He specifically referred to the Olympic flame that is kept alive so that every four years the Olympic torch can be lit to open the Olympic games. I don't really know how we got to this point, but I'm thinking that he is desperately trying to find someway to end this sermon on a positive note without really telling us the meaning of Luke's letter.

This got me to thinking on the true meaning of words. For example, Maya Angelou said "Words are things", which is to say that words can stick to walls because when you enter a room where you instantly feel comfortable, kind words have been spoken there. Likewise, if you enter a room where you feel uncomfortable from the beginning, it's probably because harmful words were exchanged in this place. I don't know if all that is true, but I think Maya is on to something because she touches nearly everyone who reads her.

Now your probably asking yourself: "How can this girl extricate herself from this mess? Doesn't she know that you can't explain a paradox by creating more contradictions?" Believe me, the thought has occurred to me . . . I remember a story that my dad told me about a book he read titled <u>Burned</u>. It was about the first slaves brought to America to work at the Antilles Trade Company. The story was universal in that people in business look for the cheapest form of labor because more production and less overhead equals more profit. The problem that occurs more often than not is that humans are greedy and they can't stand someone else being more successful than they are—so they look for ways to thwart each other's success. In the story, the Antilles Trading Company belongs to the Spanish who have all of the control but do very little of the work. The Creoles who were half European and half native decided it was time to take control, so they brought in an Englishman to train the slaves to be revolutionaries, overthrow the Spanish and take control for themselves. During this time, the Creoles would step back in and manage the land and reap the rewards; which, in a nutshell, is what the plan was from the very beginning. The problem, of course, was when the Guerrillas, who were now the rightful landowners, decided that they didn't want the Creoles in charge either. The revolutionaries began attacking the people who had put them into power in the first place. The story ends tragically when the Creoles burn the island with the rebels still on it to recapture control of their assets.

Think about this . . . the First Amendment to the Constitution of the United States protects our right to freedom of speech as long as we don't yell "Fire!" in an a crowded theater. This led me to think about two films that I recently saw. The first was "The Secret Meaning of Words" about a young woman who becomes a nurse to a man burned in an offshore drilling rig fire. At first, the young nurse, Hanna, listens to the man, Joseph, who has been temporarily blinded, spew all kinds of caustic and abusive language, which reflects his pain and bitterness in the story. She patiently endures this abuse until Joseph comes around and begins to show his human side. He tells her that he never learned how to swim. About a time when he was a little boy when his father paddled out to the middle of the lake and threw him into the water where he presumed he would drown—and about waking up in the hospital in the aftermath. He told her about falling in love with his best friend's wife and losing his best friend. Then, slowly, but surely, Hanna began to open up about her own tragic story with Joseph. About being a nursing student in the Balkans and traveling to war-torn Sarajevo on a holiday where she and her best friend were kidnapped on the road and taken hostage in a burned out hotel by soldiers of their own ethnicity. Of being raped and tortured. Of being cut open by the soldiers who proceeded to pour salt in their wounds and sewing up the wound to make them suffer even more. Toward the end of the film, Joseph is taken from the oilrig to the mainland to recover from his trauma, but it's Hanna's testimony that heals his spiritual wounds. In the denouement, Joseph reconnects with Hanna and convinces her that they were meant to be together for all time. This story made me think that it's not just the spoken word that impacts us; it's the feeling and the purpose behind the words that makes the difference.

The other film, based on a true story, was "A Peaceful Warrior" where a young man, Dan Millman, has his dream of Olympic Glory shattered by his careless and reckless attitude. He is forced to start from scratch, while employing the help of a mysterious strangers, Socrates and Joy, an elusive young woman, who systematically teach him the secrets of over-coming his weakness against incredible odds to tap into his own strength to gain wisdom and understand three un-alienable truths: "First, that change is inevitable; two, the journey is more important than the destination; and, last but never least, life is a paradox—don't try to explain it because you'll only be disappointed by the answer."

Father Mario graciously ended this conundrum by saying, "*Vayanse en paz. La misa ha terminado.*"

"*Demos gracias a dios*—Thanks be to God!"

CHAPTER 21
COMING HOME

In December of 2006, I finally came home to stay. The first thing I felt like doing was getting in touch with my old high school buddies, so I called everyone I could think of. Two numbers had been disconnected, one voice mail message and three no answers later, I decided to unpack my clothes, rearrange my room and chill. This made me remember a conversation I had with my brother-in-law about coming home at Christmas.

"How does it feel to be home Kilina?" Fernando asked.

"I don't know. A little bit strange, I guess."

"You know the good thing about being at home is that you have all of your resources at your fingertips," he paused a minute for effect. "For example—when things don't seem to be going your way, you can always take a FUBAR break and count your blessings."

""What exactly does that mean?" I asked him.

"It's an old Army term meaning Fucked Up Beyond Recognition," he laughed.

"Well, hopefully, I won't be needing to take too many of those," I added.

That led me to thinking about my dad and his uncanny way of being resourceful when it counted the most. Like the time he told my mom to keep buying gas at Frank Danna's Texaco Station—even though it was three cents more than the Mobile Station down the street.

My mother argued with him constantly, but to no avail. Three months later, California went on an odd/even license plate rationing program because of the gasoline shortage. My dad was one of the few people who could get gasoline from Mr. Danna any time he wanted it. That's the kind of person my dad was. He used to tell us it was better to be lucky than good—most days he personified that adage. I remember him telling us a time he went to *Tijuana* with his friend Ralph Inzunza to see about renting the OH! Nightclub for a Valentine's dance. They ended up at Sanborn's Café where they ordered a couple of beers. While they were there, Ralph mentioned to him that he needed to sell his house in Chula Vista because he planned to run for City Council in National City. The only problem was that Ralph needed to live in that city to file his candidacy and he couldn't afford two mortgages. My dad told him, "That's no problem—I'll buy your house!" and just like that, they shook hands on it." My mom was furious at my dad because she thought he was committing to a promise that he couldn't possibly keep. However, my dad was so sure. He never looked back—and one month from the day the two friends shook hands, we moved to our new home on Skylark Way.

Coming home, in a strange way, represented that kind of catharsis because when I was fifteen, my parents sent me to live in *Monterrey in the state of Nuevo Leon, Mexíco.* As it turned out, my ex-boyfriend wanted to pretend he was Romeo; he climbed up the tree outside my house and snuck into my bedroom through the window. That was grounds for excommunication from my mom, but my dad saw the real danger in me falling deeply in love with this gooney bird of a boyfriend. So he asked my *Tio Felipe* if I could go spend the year with them. My *Tia Blanca* worked at the school where I would attend and, by prior arrangement, my dad would send tuition money and anything else I needed right along. That year in *Monterrey* changed my life. Suddenly, I realized what a wonderful family I was born into. I spent hours at a time talking with *Sthelina,* my cousin, about all the things she knew about my dad and *Tio Felipe* when they were kids.

She treated me like the sister she never had. My dad sacrificed his whole life to make sure I had everything I needed and, often, for silly things I just wanted. In *Monterrey*, the kids had to pay for everything. They had tailor made school uniforms; they paid for books and tuition. When they got invited to a party or a dance, they had their dresses made special for the occasion. One of my classmates paid $600.00 for a dress that she wore for one party and only for a few hours—and it wasn't even the prom.

The other thing that I learned while I was in *Monterrey* was that youth is very fleeting in *México*. I saw lots of teenagers, only a couple of years older than me, who were already married and had a child. I asked my *Tio Felipe* why anyone would want to get married so young:

"You know how in the United States people start their lives at 50," he said. "It just so happens that at 50 here in *Monterrey* people begin to think about dying!"

"That's crazy," I told him.

"Yes—if you look at it from your perspective because people in the United States expect to live forever. People in *México* are not afraid of death—we just don't take life so seriously."

"Don't you think that is kind of a fatalistic attitude, tio?"

"You tell me . . . In California, people do all kind of crazy things to stay young, like plastic surgery, physical fitness, fad diets—I even hear that some people are signing up to have their body organs frozen in case they can be brought back to life . . . "

"You mean cryogenics!" I reiterated.

"Si, eso!"

"But I don't see how that's any worse than thinking about death when you're 50?"

"Ah, you've already proved my point. You see in *México*, we are not worried about growing old like you do in the U S; in fact, for us, growing old is a kind of badge of honor. To reach the ripe old age of 50 means we must have done something right. So we can actually en-joy our golden age where you spend all your time trying to recapture your youth. Now, who do you think has the advantage?"

"The jury is still out on that one, tio—but I'll admit that you have a point!"

So now that I'm home, I challenge myself to look at things from a different point of view. Mao Zedong purportedly said, "Make all things their opposite." I'm a person who was born to duality, which in essence means that I'm a product of two very different cultures. One that is very progressive, which is my American side; and the other based on years of tradition, which are my Latina roots. My American personality requires me to scrutinize everything, to be critical—even cynical at times because we believe that everyone learns from their mistakes to follow the path of success; e.g. like staying in school and getting a degree before we get married. On the opposite side, my Latina roots insist that I follow my intuition because it's more important to follow my true self. In other words, if I feel the urge to get married and have children—even if it means dropping out of school and forgoing my ambitions to raise a family, then that is what I should do! Pardon my French, but duality sucks because it means I'm only half right, and I'll always be half wrong no matter what I choose to do. So coming home means facing my reality. Don't get me wrong. I love being the person that has the opportunity to choose.

CHAPTER 22

WAR & NATIONAL SERVICE

Up until now, I haven't written anything about the war in Iraq or Afghanistan. It's not because I thought this wasn't important—not even because I was preoccupied with different endeavors. I think it has been mostly because I couldn't put my finger on what it was that I personally felt about war. Does anyone believe that Osama Bin Laden was in Iraq, or that the reason we are at war in Iraq is because Saddam Hussein was a despot? If that were the real condition for this war, every mercenary in the world would be fighting on behalf of the United States right now.

All wars are cruel. Winston Churchill once said, "The first casualty of war is the truth." So for the next half-century we probably won't know what the real reason for these conflicts are all about. My concern is this. When I look at the people in these war-torn countries, they look so much like me. That means that as long as we are fighting overseas in the Middle East, there is somebody looking at me wondering if I'm Iraqi or Afghani? It's not fair to me and it's not fair to them because, instead of thinking of me as a human being who thinks, feels, laughs and cries—we are living in constant fear of being a victim. I realize that race plays a gigantic role in our society—just like xenophobia plays a role in our economy because if I'm afraid of my neighbor, I'm willing to go to any cost to make my family safe from them. This is ludicrous when all of my energy, and half of my paycheck, go to helping me keep my peace of mind because of something I don't know, or can't understand—I'm effectively spinning my wheels in a quagmire of doubt, and that's no way to live.

Don't get me wrong. There is plenty of blame to pass around—from the President down to the Media that sensationalizes everything. The only thing I can do is to take responsibility for my own prejudice and discriminatory attitude. I have to learn to filter all of the information that comes into my brain. If someone says, "All Muslims are terrorists?" I need to ask, "Why?" If somebody else says, "It's better to be safe than sorry?" I need to respond, "To what degree?" because nothing can hurt me more than if I live in fear of not knowing what it is that I'm so afraid of; and, nothing can impact my lifestyle more than if I choose to stand by and let other people make decisions for me that I should be making for myself—that's just the way it is and the way it's meant to be.

At least half the people in the United States right now have become complacent with the way they live. Why? Mostly because it doesn't cost us anything but our own self-determination and our civil liberties. We have all kind of learned to take these things for granted because we inherited them from our predecessors. We never had our sovereignty challenged or had to live under a dictatorship—that is, until now. We always thought that we were "One nation, under God with liberty and justice for all." Even when we recognized that not everyone in our neighborhood had the same lifestyle, or the same commodities we did—we just figured it was because we were more industrious, more blessed, or less careless than everyone else. Well, guess what? We've become consumers of what everyone else in the world produces. It's like 89% of our gross national product is outsourced to other developing countries. What is it that we produce? Some people believe it's communication technology. Even when a lot of European countries see us as a beacon of opportunity because of their restrictive policies that prohibit new industries, we can't take advantage of our own resources because we don't know how, or refuse to work for substandard wages according to our lifestyle. Now, when you call a credit card company, someone in India or Pakistan picks up the phone to ask how they can help you. We effectively consume most of what other countries make and we have forgotten how to be self-reliant. Ralph Waldo Emerson said, "Consistency is the hobgoblin of little minds." I think what he was telling us was that when you do the same thing consistently, you will always get the same result. Therefore, it's time that we wake up from our slumber and put our initiative and common sense to work. We can NO longer be at war with ourselves in terms of gobbling up what the rest of the world produces. We have the resources and the energy—we need to make a place that is friendlier toward our neighbors and ourselves by consuming less and producing more, so that our sons and daughters can be at peace with the world and not consumed by it.

"One time I asked my dad, "Why do countries go to war?"

"I don't really know, Love . . . probably because it's easier than trying to work out a compromise with each other," he said.

"Then why don't nations hire a consultant, or a mediator like people do when they want to settle a disagreement—so they can negotiate an amicable settlement?"

"It certainly sounds reasonable to me, but 'amicable' is often synonymous with losing—and most leaders are afraid of being labeled losers."

"How can they be labeled losers when both sides win?"

"Go figure! Maybe you should go into politics, Kilina?"

"I don't think I would last very long, dad."

"You've got my vote whenever you decide to launch you candidacy!"

"At the end of the day we have more similarities than differences, so why shouldn't we learn to compromise and get along."

"Say 'Amen!' to that."

So what would a plan for a universal national service look like? Basically, it would be voluntary because we are living in "the land of the free." In my dad's time, we had something called the Draft where people were remanded to do military service; until, of course, people decided that it was unconstitutional. Then there was something called the Lottery where people under 19 were given a number, which took them into the Vietnam War—that too was declared unconstitutional. Now we have a voluntary Army, but the only people that volunteer are the people who are forced by their circumstances to join the military.

I read an article in <u>Time</u> Magazine by Richard Stengel and it made a lot of sense to me. He says that he would institute a ten-point plan that would put America back on its feet. First, he would give each new born baby in the United States an endowment of $5000.00 which would stay in the bank until the child was 18 years, or old enough for national service. At the rate of about 7% this would become $19,000.00 by the time this young person is old enough to volunteer. Since it's strictly voluntary, the person doesn't have to access this stipend; however, it's one hell of an incentive plan—don't you think? The really cool thing is that it would only cost about 4 billion dollars to do this, which according to Stengel, " . . . is about the cost of what two months of war in Iraq costs us now, or one half of what we spend per year in our penal system." In addition, the government would recuperate one billion dollars in dividends from the people that volunteer, and all of the money from the people who don't.

Some of these ideas seem substantially advantageous. For example, instead of the volunteer Corporation for National and Community Service, we could have a Cabinet level appointment that would command both the respect and the interest of the young people. There would be goals and objectives, the government would be held accountable, and it would become part of every politician's platform. Instead of a "War on Terror", or a "War on Poverty" we could have young people enthusiastic about making our country better.

Secondly, it would encourage the expansion of programs like Americorps, a tutoring and educational service for the most effected urban areas, which includes after-school programs, playground renovations, the construction of new recreational facilities and care for the elderly. According to the data, 24 hours after Katrina hit the Gulf Coast, Americorps was there to help; and they since have contributed over three million hours of community service to restore New Orleans and the surrounding areas. It wouldn't necessarily take responsibility away from the National Guard or the government, but a voluntary national service program would certainly instill civic and national pride in this type of work.

When I was in high school, we had a program called AVID, which is an acronym for Advancement Via Individual Determination. The lifeblood of this program was the college tutors who knew a little bit about every subject that we studied in high school. Think about what that would mean to the underachieving students if we had a cadre of tutors who were paid a small stipend by the government with the promise of fully paid tuition to the college or university of their choice. Obviously, all students need some kind of remuneration for their services; however, most college students relish the opportunity to show us what they know. I think just having someone who can help you solve problems when you need a friend is an invaluable resource all by itself.

The next area that a universal national service program would help with is immigration. Think about it—college level students could help undocumented people apply for residency when it's applicable. Also, they could help the elderly and people of limited resources apply for health care if necessary. There would also be opportunities to show what they know. I think that just having someone who can help you solve a problem when you need a friend is an invaluable resource.

There would also be an opportunity for these young people to travel to foreign countries to expand programs like the Peace Corps and VISTA. There is no end to the good things that a universal national service program could do. The total number of service hours would more than compensate the government's initial investment. It's a win/win situation.

When you talk about drawbacks, I really can't think of any—although I know that skeptics abound. I suppose some politicians will say a national service program will thwart young people's initiative to volunteer on their own, or perhaps to do paid fellowships at the university that could potentially be more rewarding for them individually. The problem from my point of view is that when you focus more on the rewards, the less we are able to concentrate on the prize, which is the gift of giving our time and energy to making the world a better place to live for everyone.

CHAPTER 23

MONA

SHORTLY AFTER I CAME HOME, we lost our dog Cookie, a Japanese Chin because she got a chicken bone stuck in her throat. At the same time, a close friend, Maggie Pereyra, was moving to Edinburg, Texas and needed a place to leave their Saint Bernard, 'Mona'. My dad had always wanted a St. Bernard—ever since we could remember, so Maggie told us we could keep her, a tri-colored ball of fluff, until her husband could make arrangements for her in their new home.

I loved the dog at first glance because it kind of filled the void my dad left when he died. Karina loved her too because she was good therapy for our family. The first thing we did was buy a leash to take Mona running *in Los Niños* Park behind our house. A couple of times my mom tried to walk her, but when Mona saw a cat or another dog, she lit out after them dragging my mom behind. Mona was good-natured and spent most of her time in our backyard sleeping. However, when a stranger, like Santos the gardener, came in the gate, her ears would perk up and she would start barking. I spent hours at a time combing her hair and talking to the dog about everything—mostly about how my dad would take her for long walks on the beach if he were here. Mona just put her head down with her sad eyes, looked up and listened. Whenever we went shopping these days, we would have to make an unsolicited stop in the pet aisle to find some special treat for Mona.

Now a couple of times, Mona got out of the yard without her leash, but she always came back. Most of all, she just wanted Karina or me to go chase her; however, when we sat back down exhausted from running around, Mona would politely walk back to us and lay her head on the ground next to us. The only real problem with Mona was that she seemed to keep getting ear infections regularly, which meant another trip to the vet. The veterinarian always gave her an antibiotic shot and some drops to go in her ears and send her home. Mona didn't want anyone getting near her ears. She would flop them back and forth frantically until we were through giving her the drops, or we would give up trying to apply the medication.

Then, one day, Maggie's husband José called from McAllen, Texas and said he had a dream about my dad. In the dream my dad told him to give me the dog because I really needed it. José woke up in a cold sweat that night because he said that it felt like a premonition. He said he had never had anything like that happen to him before. The very next morning he called our home to give me the NEWS. At first, I felt overwhelmed at the idea of having Mona on a full time basis as my responsibility, but then I realized that's what my dad wanted me to do and that made it all right. From that day on, I would walk Mona through the park every day I was home. Sometimes Kariff would come over and we would go running to kill two birds with one stone. I would always tell Mona stories about things I did with my dad while he was still alive. Mona would listen attentively; then, a cat or dog walking by would distract her and we were off to the races.

It was a chilly night in October when my mom accidently left the garage door open while she was talking to our neighbor, Maria Elena Ruiz from across the street. Mona seized the opportunity to quietly trot out into the front yard and then, without even looking both ways, across the street. She was careful to sniff and mark her territory as she passed from one yard to the next. Maggie who was visiting at the time, yelled at my mom to tell her that Mona had escaped to which she replied: "She's done it before, she'll come back home when she gets tired exploring!" But she didn't come back right away. Instead, she pried open the gate at the Winkowski's and grabbed Simba their 14-year-old Yorkshire terrier. By the time I got there, it was too late. Mona had chewed Simba nearly in half trying to protect him from the neighbors who were frantically trying to pull him from her jaws.

"*Quitale el perro!*" my mom yelled out mortified.

"*No puedo, mama!* I can't get him away!" I yelled back. Mona just shook her head in disagreement to whatever we said and Simba held on for his dear life. Maggie tried hitting Mona on the head with a plastic whiffle bat, Maria Elena tried twisting her tail, but nothing seemed to work.

From a distance, Ray Winkowski saw what was going on and told his wife Angie to fetch him some rubber gloves from his workshop: "The purple ones from the shelf next to the cabinets," he told her. When Angie returned with the gloves, he calmly fit one of the gloves on to his left hand as he walked towards the melee with Mona. When he reached our front yard, he told Maria Elena to hold Mona's tail in the air, he stuck his middle three fingers up Mona's behind. At that instant, Mona's jaw dropped and Simba fell to the ground.

I was horrified almost as much as my mom. Angie and my mom rushed Simba to the all night veterinarian hospital, but Simba had too many internal wounds and lacerations and he had to be put to sleep. Mom talked to me about Mona. Maggie insisted that it wasn't Mona's fault and that we would just have to be more careful in the future—but we all realized she had to go because nobody in our small neighborhood would feel comfortable around her any more. Both Karina and I cried the day they took Mona away to her new family in Guadalajara.

CHAPTER 24

STUMBLING

REMEMBER what Olivia said about Roy? Well, she was right! After our initial meeting, I met Roy a few more times. All of them were very casual and uncompromising, but this one time, I stumbled.

"Roy, I'm not a very good girl," I told him.

"Why do you say that, Kilina?" he asked me.

"For one reason, I already have a boyfriend . . ."

"I know—you mean Kariff?" he muttered still somewhat miffed.

"I mean, I'm starting to have feelings for you," I told him.

"And why is that a bad thing?" Roy mused.

"Because you and I aren't meant to be," I said.

"How do you know that?"

"It's kind of hard to explain, but if there is one thing I learned from my dad—it's how to be loyal," I said with my fingers crossed behind my back.

"Then why are you here?" he said with a hint of sarcasm.

I thought about that for a moment and I began to think about my answer. It would be so easy to blame my mom for this because she was only loyal to her biological family—not to my dad and not to me. Then, again, that was a cop out and nothing is that easy. So I thought about Kariff. What bugged me about him was that he was so jealous of everyone. If there was one thing I could change about Kariff, it was just that. I wanted him to trust me for who I am—deliberately and unquestionably. I thought about how I deserved to be trusted. I had not been with another guy since I told Kariff we might as well be boyfriend and girlfriend since we were always together. That didn't mean that I wasn't tempted once in awhile. It just meant that I had never been unfaithful to him—now I had the opportunity and the desire.

"I suspect because I want to know what it's like to be on the other side of the looking glass. I want to know what it feels like to be a guy."

Without even pausing to ask, Roy bent down and kissed me on the lips. I didn't flinch; in fact, it felt kind of nice for a change. There was no urgency in his kiss. No guilt. We stayed there wrapped up in the moment with each other, without speaking and I could hear the rustling of the leaves on the ground; a solitary bird chirping in the tree next to us. I could feel the warmth of the sunshine on my neck and time stood still because *alegria* is a habit that is made one moment at a time.

After what seemed to be an eternity, Roy broke the silence, "Why is it so important for you to do things the way your parents, or maybe just the way your dad wanted you to?"

I don't have a pat answer for you—if that's what you're looking for? My dad used to say it was an intuitive thing for him; he instinctively knew when things felt right or wrong. It was easy for him to choose the right path because of it."

"I get it that you feel like you owe your dad to do the right thing, but who is to say that you and I aren't made to be together?" Roy inquired.

"That's the trick! If we were meant to be together, there would be NO questioning. There would be NO guilt feelings; in fact, there probably be NO conversation. See my dad thought that you could question how a person thought about a situation. What you couldn't do was question the way a person felt—that was just wrong because a person doesn't choose to feel good or bad. They just do! My mom argued with him that we have a choice about feeling the way we feel. That was because her parents often told her how she should feel; especially when it came to feeling guilty. Not my dad. Too many times there was nobody around to tell him anything, so he had to adlib the script the way he felt. He came to the conclusion that you can't make stuff up. There has to be a higher order that dictates the way you feel—so that's what he did."

"I feel like I would have liked to have met your dad!" Roy said firmly with tongue-in-cheek.

"I think he would have felt good about meeting you too."

Roy and I spent the day together. We walked several miles around Sea Port Village. We ate and we talked. We promised each other to pursue the question of our friendship more in the future, but we never did. I think about Roy often because he made me think about my feelings, which is something I didn't like doing before because it was always painful; but, now that I understand myself more, I'll try to do it more often. Most of all, I learned from Roy that if it can't endure questioning, if it can't be subjected to the truth, then it's probably not worth the effort. So real feelings have to be subjected to this line of inquiry. How do you feel about them apples?

CHAPTER 25

FLEAS & PIKE

PERHAPS THE MOST INTERESTING class I took once I got to San Diego State was Education 401 with Dr. René Nuñez. Dr. Nuñez looked like a cross between Albert Einstein and Harpo Marx with his grey Afro haircut. He was actually one of the eleven that were indicted for the high school walkouts back in the '70s. When he taught his class, he could speak from experience about what it's like to feel isolated in your classroom or singled out by the FBI as a loose cannon or a rabble-rouser.

The introduction to Dr. René's class was about 'Fleas & Pike'. According to the good doctor, we are all creatures of habit; once we have established a ritual, our habits pretty much dictate our lives. Everyone has heard about the circus elephant that can pull a tree from its roots with one tug. However, when the elephant was just a baby, the trainer tied him to a peg and, no matter how hard the little elephant tried to tear away, he always ended up frustrated and raveled up in the cord at the stake. So, after a while, the elephant quit trying to get loose. René claimed that as humans, we are the same way.

For the first example, Dr Nuñez used the same circus motif with the trainer who makes the fleas do tricks. For example, everyone knows that fleas are born to jump, so the trainer puts them in a matchbox and every time they jump, they get a headache. After awhile, the fleas stop jumping, so the trainer can make them do things they won't ordinarily do—so they won't get a headache. The professor suggests that this is what happens to us when we are in elementary school. As long as we perform to the teacher's expectations, we get a star on the forehead and a satisfactory written on our progress report. On the contrary, if we don't perform to expectations and we do something that is out of the norm, we get time out and we learn the message that we need to do things differently.

On the very first day of class, a girl by the name of Carmen came in late. Naturally, Dr. Nuñez questioned her tardiness: "Why are you so late? Didn't you get the syllabus that said we start promptly at 9:00 AM?"

The girl, who appeared a little bit stunned, answered him: "Dr. Nuñez, I wear braces on both of my knees because I was diagnosed with *thrombophlebitis* at birth, and because I was not aware that I had to climb 102 stairs to get to your class—that's why I'm late!"

I doubt that he even knew what her disease was, but René turned to us with a sly grin while crossing his arms and he said: "Do you believe this excuse? Young lady, I'm not going to excuse you for having braces on your legs; neither am I going to exonerate you for what you don't know. Tomorrow I expect you to get here when the class starts on time—do I make myself understood?"

Everyone looked at René a little surprised, like this girl didn't deserve this diatribe on punctuality. After all, it was only the first day, but that's just the beginning of the story.

As the class went on, according to Dr. Nuñez, when we want to get into good habits, we always need to do four things to be successful. In the order of their importance, we need to have DESIRE, the OPPORTUNITY, the KNOWLEDGE and the ABILITY; otherwise, we will never get into the habit. The first principle, DESIRE is obvious. If we don't have the will to do something, the chances are slim to none that we will be successful at it. Secondly, we must have the OPPORTUNITY because, if we don't put ourselves into a position to have the experience, we will never have the chance to gain wisdom from it. Thirdly, we must have some KNOWLEDGE—some basic information about the habit we want to create. Without this, we will effectively be spinning our proverbial wheels in the quick sand because it won't happen. Finally, according to Nuñez, we must have the ABILITY to pursue our goal because you wouldn't ask a child to walk if they haven't learned to crawl. I thought I saw Carmen cringe at this last remark. Given these four essential factors, a person must be able to practice their task before it can become a habit. Then he turned the conversation back on Carmen: "Do you agree with this assessment young lady, or do you have some alternative strategy that we can benefit from?"

"Dr, Nuñez, if you don't want me in your class, why don't you just say so—I can leave right now!" She said.

From the expression on René's face, I could tell he was up to something, but none of us had a clue what it was: "No! I want you to stay!" he told her, "but I still want you to be on time tomorrow!" That was the end of the class the first day.

※ ※

The next day, Dr. Nuñez told us the story about the pike. As luck would have it, the pike is a fish that feeds on other types of fishes. When the pike is inserted into a fish tank by itself and placed adjacent to another fish tank with smaller fish, it will try unsuccessfully to catch and eat the other fish. Until, one day, it will stop trying. On that day, you can mix the fish together in one tank since the pike will no longer be a threat to the other fish.

This is what Dr. Nuñez claimed happens to the majority of college students. They are all little fish in the big pond with the pike. They try unsuccessfully to succeed on their own, until the time when they finally learn that they can't be successful—no matter how hard they try. Many learn to get through it by the skin of their teeth; and, others just give up trying. According to him, good study habits come from trying again and again until you get it right. Statistically, the failure rate for the average incoming freshman class at the university is around 70%. Nuñez told us. "Thomas Edison said ' . . .every time he failed at something, he was much closer to being successful because he knew one more way that didn't work.' So he could eliminate that strategy from his repertoire."

This time it was Carmen's turn to ask a question: "It sounds like a big fish story to me!" We all laughed. "What does a pike, or a little fish in a big pond have to do with anything! I don't get this analogy," she said.

"Well, check it out. How is all this relevant you ask? First of all, I spent twenty years applying to get my doctorate at this university. Every year, I was turned down and encouraged to try again the following year . . . College is not about who is the smartest or the most motivated because, if that were the case, I would have given up at the beginning. The spoils go to the person who is the most persistent! I learned perseverance—along the way, if I always approached getting my degree the same way, I would always be rejected. The day I decided to pick up the peg, look for the light at the end of the match box, and jump into the next fish tank is the day I was successful at becoming the person I always wanted to be."

Carmen looked as if she had been harpooned, but that didn't stop her from asking Dr. Nuñez questions, especially about the chapter "Self-Help in Hard Times" from the textbook we were reading called Howard Zinn's The People's History of the United States. Dr. Nuñez also shared something called "The Line of Inequity" and told us that we tend to pre-judge each other because that's the way our brain works. We seldom get to learn about each other outside of class, so he took us outside to do the exercise. The Line of Inequity helped to explode the myths by showing us how the people we think are the most privileged seldom are. For example, Carmen actually ended up in the front of the line because with her disability, people often felt sorry for her and gave her special attention—something Dr. Nuñez refused to do. It made me cry when I saw a lot of the friends I had made in class end up at the back of the line. Even though I ended up somewhere in the middle, I felt spoiled rotten that day.

René Nuñez taught us many lessons, especially about being human and showing us compassion for each other. However, the real miracle happened at the end of the class when Carmen, who had worn the prosthesis since she was a child, walked out of the doctor's class without her braces—and never wore them again.

CHAPTER 26

FRIENDSHIP

Toward the end of Fannie Flagg's novel <u>Fried Green Tomatoes</u>, the main character answers the question to "What's the most important thing in life?" The answer is "Friendship." I believe in this axiom for several good reasons.

We don't get to pick our family members. Our brothers and sisters often fail to meet with our own personal expectations of what a good friend should be. Melody is both my sister and my best friend because she is always looking out for me; however, because she is my sister first, there are things that we can't agree on, like how to remember our dad. Melody's experience with dad is a lot different then mine. She felt like my dad let her down when he supported my mom defending my grandfather because he didn't speak up, or take any action against our grandfather. My point of view is that he had a difficult choice between going to war, or keeping the peace with my mother's brother and sisters—he chose the peaceful option; but this particular anecdote is more family history and less about friendship.

One of the things that prevents Melody and me from being closer is the big/little sister relationship. An example of this would be when she calls me the night before a scholarship application is due: "Kilina—I need you to fill out the application I'm e-mailing to you. Attach your résumé and your autobiographical essay to it. The deadline is tomorrow night."

"How am I supposed to get everything together by tomorrow night?"

"I know you will find a way. Besides you already have most of this stuff on a PDF file. All you have to do is print it out," she rationalized.

"You know what—I'll do it, but, next time, could you give me a little advanced notice?"

"Hey! The scholarship is for you—not me! If you don't want to do it . . ."

"You know I love you, Melody!"

All of a sudden, instead of "This is an incredible opportunity for you!" it becomes, "I'm your BIG sister and I know what's best for you!"

One of my very best friends is Ana Figueroa. Why? Quite simply—because she is so loyal to me. When I went away to Monterrey for a year, Sthelina was my confidant, but Ana sent me an e-mail nearly every day—just to keep me up to date on all of the gossip that was happening at Chula Vista High School. When I came home, she was one of the first people to come around to visit me and she never left. Even when I moved to Long Beach to go to college, she called me every other day. A typical conversation between Ana and me would sound like this: "So what are you going to dress up as for Halloween?"

"How should I know? We just celebrated Valentine's Day! Why are you worried about Halloween?"

"It's just that I saw these really cute wings that I thought we could dress up like pixies . . ."

"Ana—only you could think up stuff like that!"

The other thing about Ana is that there is never a dull moment with this girl because she is such a drama queen:

"Kilina—I think I lost my cell phone again?"

"What else is new? How many times have you lost it—this month already?" I asked.

"My dad is going to kill me because it's a company phone!"

"So what do you want me to do about it?"

"Well, maybe you could call him and tell him that I left it at your house and you misplaced it or something?"

"Ana, that would be lying to your dad. I really don't want to go there!"

"Please—I promise I won't ask you for another favor this year!"

"Yeah, right! More like for the rest of this week," I said.

"That's why you're my best bud!"

One of the fallacies about friendship is that friends will never exploit you. Guess what? It's quite common for your friends to take advantage of you when they need a favor, like Kariff for instance:

"Kilina, do you think we can take your sister Karina to the movies with us?"

"I guess so, but why do you want to take my sister with us?"

"She has a handicapped placard—doesn't she?"

"Duh, yeah! Why do we need a handicapped placard?"

"Well, I kind of got a ticket for parking in a handicapped zone without a permit."

"Jeez! I wonder why anyone would give you a ticket for that?" I asked sarcastically.

"You've got to help me because the ticket is $550.00. If I can prove that I had a handicapped permit, but I forgot to put it on the car mirror, it'll only cost $125.00. You think your sister can help us out?"

"I'll ask her, but if my parents find out, they'll blow a gasket. You better let me handle it with my sister."

Don't get me wrong, there is nothing wrong about helping out a friend; but, sometimes, helping out can be sticky business. Like when my friend Jenn told her mom she was going to be at my house, so she could spend the night with her boyfriend. That night her mom called me to ask me the question:

"Is Jennifer there with you, Kilina?"

"Uh, no!" I lamented my answer as soon as I gave it.

"Has she been there and gone somewhere else?"

"Did she tell you she was coming to my house?"

"That would be the reason I'm calling your house, yes!"

"You know what? I haven't seen her, but maybe she just didn't get here yet!" I told her.

"Don't try to cover for her. If she's not there, she's probably not going to get there anytime soon. It's already 11:30 PM."

The Jenn's mom abruptly hung up the phone on me. What was even more perplexing, however, was the next day when Jenn called me:

"Hey, homegirl, how come you didn't cover for me with my mom last night?"

"Jenn—how was I supposed to cover for you when I didn't even know you told your mom you were with me?"

"I always cover for you. You couldn't return the favor?"

"I beg to differ with you. First of all, when have I ever lied to my parents so you could protect me?"

"That's my whole point—you never want to anything for me. You're always thinking about yourself!"

"A friend once told me that what other people say about you has more to do with them, how they think about things, than it does about me. I think that principle applies here—don't you think?" I said in a matter-of-fact tone.

"Well, I just called to let you know that my mom said that I won't be able go stay at your house anymore."

"Okay—and how is that my fault?"

"It's just that she realized that you're not as good of friend as she thought you were for me."

"You know what? If that's the way your mom thinks, she's certainly entitled to her opinion—that's fine with me!"

"FINE!" then she hung up.

The reason I wrote about Jenn is that it's a perfect example of how friends exploit each other, or try to anyway. It's not necessarily because we don't value our friends; it's more because we want to trust them to do the right thing by us, and we can't see past the forest for the trees at times, which brings me to the pinnacle story of friendship.

One time while I was still in middle school, my friend Ashley and I were at Wal-Mart when we decided that we needed some fresh makeup. Now when you're 13 or 14, the last things you think about are consequences. So we promptly began to unwrap what we wanted and stuck it into our purses. It never in a thousand years occurred to us that they had surveillance cameras recording our every move. Subsequently, we reached the exit door, and before we could breath a collective sigh of relief, the security guard stopped us and asked us to empty our bags out on his table. We began by arguing that the merchandise in our possession had been purchased on a previous trip to Wal-Mart; however, by this time, we had been shuffled off to the back room where we could watch ourselves shoplifting on videotape. Ashley whispered under her breath, "I didn't think they even kept film in those cameras!"

The store manager gave us an ultimatum, "Either your parents come down to pick you up and pay for the merchandise, or I call the police to come to write you up for shoplifting and you go to Juvy!"

It really wasn't an option, although Ashley was unable to get a hold of her parents, when I called home, I expected to talk to my dad, but my mom was the only one there:

"Hi, mom . . . is dad at home?" I must have sounded kind of anxious.

"No! He hasn't come home yet. *Que tienes?* What seems to be the problem?" she said inquisitively.

"Mom—Ash and I are being detained at Wal-Mart because they say we were shoplifting makeup . . ." I had trouble finishing the sentence.

"Uh-huh, just what do you expect your father to do?" she said abruptly.

"Mom—if you don't come get us in a half-an-hour, they are going to arrest us," I spoke with more urgency now.

"Maybe you should have thought about that before you helped yourself to their makeup," she scolded while stating the obvious.

"Mom—will you please come and get us," I cried.

"I'll be there when I get there," was all she said.

We waited for what seemed like an eternity, but she came. She talked to the store manager alone. Then she paid for the merchandise, which she promptly left at the register. Finally, she turned to us and asked: "Are you young ladies ready to go home now?"

My punishment was that I couldn't go anywhere with my friends, or by myself, for the next six months. In addition, I had to pay my mom back for the makeup she deliberately left at Wal-Mart. The manager told her they would have a restraining order to arrest us if we came anywhere near the store. Nonetheless, the reason I remembered the story was because my mom was there for me when I needed her most. Ashley's parents never even showed to pick her up. Some friends are good at getting you into trouble, but only your best friend will get you out.

CHAPTER 27
SPIRITUALITY

THERE IS A BOOK called <u>The Passion Test</u> by Janet Bray Attwood, and after I read it, I made the following assessment of spirituality. Basically, the premise is that "If you are true to yourself, and you do everything you can do to follow your dreams; then, in the end, you should have no remorse."

Janet Attwood talks about meeting Dr. Pankaj Naram who introduced her to the Aghori Master who told her story after story of "letting man/woman seek realization of self." When she asked the Aghori what more she needed to know about herself, he told her: "You are not your body!" Having traveled throughout India where, at times, her body suffered from vomiting, diarrhea and headaches, she thought: "Thank goodness I'm not my body!" On a deeper level, she came to understand what led her to the discovery of an answer that had intrigued her: That her reality transcended the physical form of her body.

Janet tells the story of her step-mom, Margie, who needed her help at precisely the moment she was planning to leave for India to fulfill her lifelong plan to meet the Aghori and other saints. She talked about how this brief interruption in her plans was actually a blessing because it provided her the opportunity to be with a loved one in the most critical time of their existence. Later, it provided her with the experience to share with one of the saints, which led her to the discovery of an answer that had intrigued her for most of her adult life: "Why do bad things happen to good people?"

At one point in her journey, she stayed with the saint Bapuji in India. As luck would have it, she accidentally started a fire that burned the guesthouse and everything in it. She was totally humbled and remorseful; however, Bapuji and his family laughed and rejoiced that she had been a part of this occasion because it was an opportunity to cleanse themselves of 'worldly' possessions that were obstructing them from their true calling of being helpful to each other. Janet says the lesson she learned from this was, "Be alert! Sometimes the good coming to you may be disguised as something uncomfortable or undesirable . . . When this happens, stay open to see where the good is coming from within the discomfort."

This led me to another revelation, which is an allegory about the slave who disobeys his master. It happened to this king had everything except spirituality. One day, the king told his slave to prepare to go on a hunting trip with him, but the slave, because he had a premonition the night before, told the king there would be a regretful event during this hunting trip, so he begged the king not to go. The king stubbornly persisted, but the slave refused to budge, so the king threw him in the dungeon and proceeded with the expedition. The first day out, the king accidentally severed his finger with his hunting knife and thought ill of his slave as if somehow he had caused this event to happen. Upon returning to the castle, the king was captured by a tribe of natives who took the king to be sacrificed before their deity. When they realized the king was missing his middle finger, they promptly let him go because he was NOT perfect enough to sacrifice him to their god. Subsequently, the king returned home and released the slave from the dungeon and asked him the following: "I understand now that your God must be powerful because he warned you of what would happen on the hunting expedition; but if he is really so powerful, why did he allow me to throw you into the dungeon?"

"It's very simple," the slave answered. "If I had been with you,

I was not missing any fingers, so I would have been the one to be sacrificed!"

So all of this brought me to thinking about losing my dad and what that meant to me. First of all, I never spent one wasted moment with my dad. We were always talking about stuff, sometimes trivial things but there was never any time that wasn't fruitful in some way, shape or form. I remember a time when I asked my dad why he married my mom since she wasn't of his same social status and his parents were against them getting married in the first place. This is what he told me:

"To me your mom was the most beautiful girl in the world. When she smiled, the whole world lit up for me."

"Dad—I think you were imagining things because I've never seen anyone light up around mom because she made them happy. Maybe because she pissed them off!"

"Actually, the spark that I saw in your mom is in you, Kilina. I see it every day and you light up the room around you where ever you go." This made me blush.

"Gracias por el piropo! Thank you for the compliment, but I get the sense that you and mom are not always on the same page—and that causes you a lot of anxiety."

"You're right about that, but—you know what? I don't regret a single moment with your mom because she makes me feel alive!"

"How so?"

"Someone much wiser than me said, 'The most important thing about feeling pain is that it brings about the recognition that you're very much alive.' Did you know that some psychologists say that the center of pain and pleasure are located in the same place in our brain? Plus, when you NO longer feel anything—you're probably dead!" We both laughed at this revelation.

So you're probably wondering, 'What does this have to do with spirituality?' Simply, what we think, what we believe, what other people say or tell us are all things that take place in our mind; however, what we feel, what we know intuitively will always take place in our heart, which is closer to the truth of who we are and how we are connected to god and the universe. Losing my dad was the most devastating experience of my life, but he has never left my heart. I know now that every decision I make, everything I do is because the love we have for each other transcends this world.

I know that some day someone will read this and think to themselves: "This girl has lost her bats from the belfry!" That's okay. According to Janet Attwood and her collaborators, "We are all made from love." That's where I'm coming from and where I want to be.

EPILOG

TODAY WAS MY FIRST DAY of teaching at my old stomping grounds, Rohr Elementary School. You know we all "ROHR" like lions here. I don't know quite what to expect, but I do know that I'm going to have a good day because my dad is watching over me. It's kind of ironic knowing that I've traveled so far away to come home, but I know now that I'm where I belong.

Math, science and reading were all by the book, so I'm looking forward to the children's writing because we finally get the chance to be creative, which is just plain fun. When I gave this assignment to my second graders during student teaching, we had a blast. The task was to take an every day saying, or slogan, and fill in the blanks with their own words or ideas; for example, Betty Young wrote, "It's better to be late . . . than pregnant."

Liz Villagran said, "Whatever shivers . . . must have forgotten to wear a sweater."

Mari Velasquez wrote, "A fool and his money . . . have a lot of fun spending it."

Pancho Gonzalez said, "The early bird usually . . . goes to bed by eight o'clock."

Erika Vargas offered, "He who finds a good shade tree . . . probably doesn't live in the desert."

Pedro Anaya shared, "Early to bed, early to rise makes . . . it hard to stay up past your bedtime."

Karla Ramirez wrote, "You will never know . . . until you check your horoscope on the Internet."

Gerardo Bermudez said, "In between a rock . . . and roll paradise."

Patty Muñoz wrote, "Better safe . . . than getting a ticket in the fast lane."

José Medrano offered, "If there is one thing I know . . . it's my teacher makes my day seem eternal."

Adriana Inzunza said, "A penny saved . . . doesn't help you at the gas pump."

Terrance Smith wrote, "Easy come . . . when you know where it's coming from."

Andrea Martinez shared, "With money . . . we will all go out dancing on Saturday night."

Finally, *Benita Viramontes*said, "Love makes . . . a lot of money on Valentine's Day."

Speaking of love . . . I always thought that everyone's goal in life was to find true love. My parents pretty much cemented that idea for me because they spent eleven years as *novios*, or sweethearts, then 35 years as husband and wife. Nevertheless, my dad said "Life isn't always a bowl of cherries." So it got me to thinking, there has to be something more than love that people care about. As life would have it, there is! It's called the pursuit of happiness because happiness, or *alegria* as it's called in my native language, is the presence of God in all of us. My dad had it, my mom has it—and I'm pretty sure I inherited it from them. It's not a big revelation, but it was an important one for me because I understand my destiny and what my goal in life must be. It's all I ever cared about and it's what I want from life. They say it's not the destination but the journey that counts. If that's the case, I'm on my way.

The day my dad died, I stopped pursuing happiness because I somehow thought God was punishing me for the way that I think, or maybe something that I said. Now that I have finished writing this story, I'm really going to get it! Now, slowly but surely, I'm coming to the realization that death is not a punishment for anything—it's just another part of life. The people that come and go in our lives have a mission to fulfill the same as we do. Some of them finish their job sooner; some of us take a little longer to do it. When we have completed out time here on Earth, we need to move on *porque la vida es tan corta.* I would like to think that some day my time will come. My dad will be there on the other side waiting to tell me: "At the end of the day, even in the darkest of times, you can find *alegria* in the light of the smallest candle."

Fin